Lovers & Losses

B. Heather Mantler

Lit-N-Laughter

ISBN:1927507197
ISBN-13:9781927507193
Library and Archives Canada Cataloguing in Publication
Mantler,   B.   Heather,   1987-,   author
Lovers & losses / B. Heather Mantler.
  ISBN 978-1-927507-19-3 (paperback)
  I. Title. II. Title: Lovers and losses.
PS8626.A676L68 2015 C813'.6 C2015-905767-1

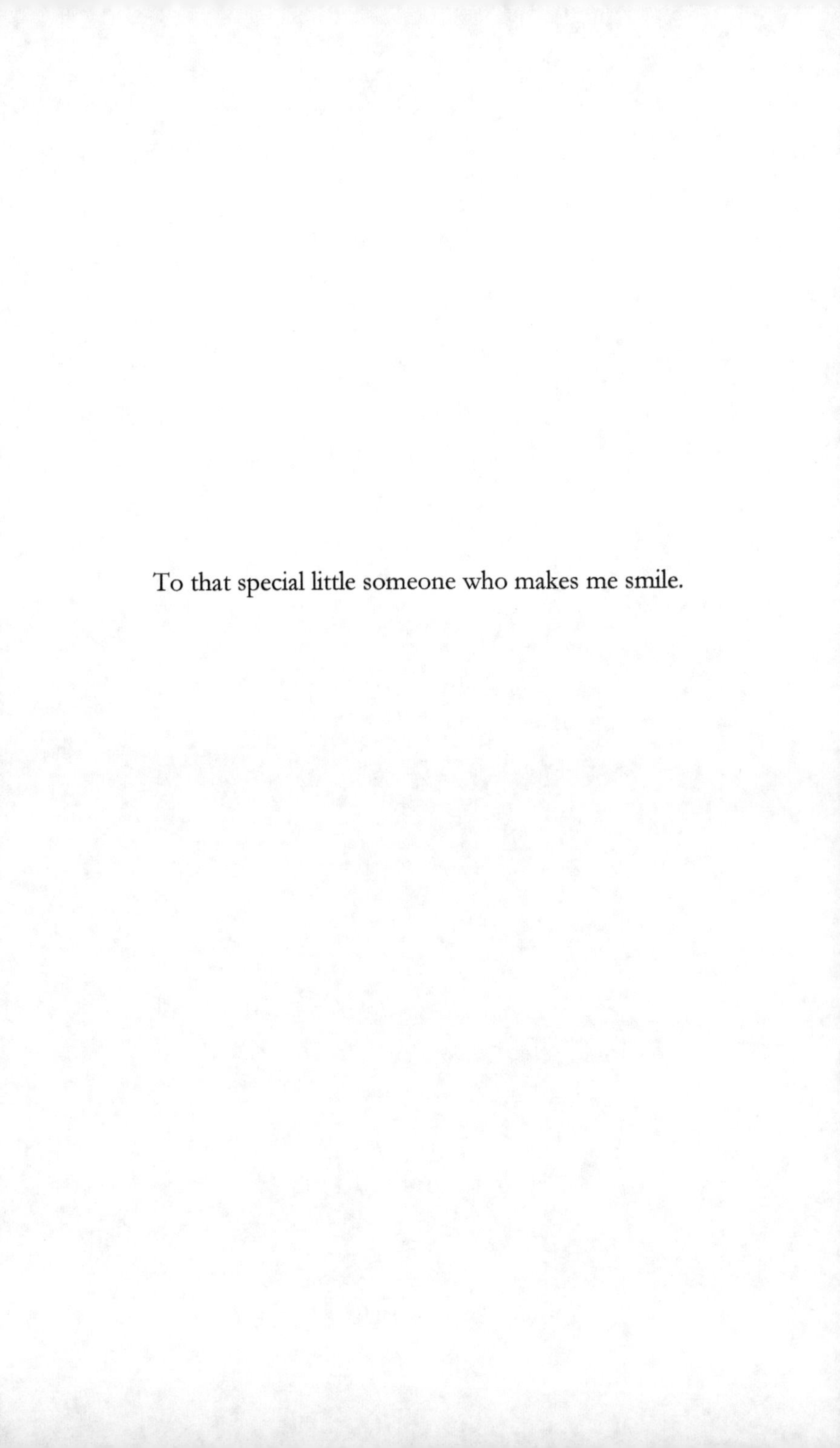

To that special little someone who makes me smile.

RANA WANTS TO AVOID A SCANDAL AND
HIDE HER NEW SECRET

Lady Rana of Proster sighed as she watched the magician, Luce, walk out the courtyard gates. He had taken everything with him except two things. One-half of her heart and the child she had not had time to tell him about. She had only found out she was with child this morning, but she had not been able to talk to him, or send him a message. He was now beyond her range, and she did not know where to send the message as she did not know his destination. She had to accept that he was gone and think about what she was going to do. She could not stay at court because that would cause a scandal among the nosy members of the court though neither her brother nor Hillel would be bothered that she had gotten herself pregnant without having a husband. Weldon would be concerned about whether she was taken care of, whereas Hillel did not care at all.

Rana turned back to the door of the castle. Only a few others had come out to see Luce off and they had already gone off to their duties. Rana was alone as she went back inside out of the chilly spring wind. The hallway had servants, but no one else. There was no court today, upper or lower. None of the servants stopped Rana as she swept through the hallway and up the stairs. She went straight to the library, which was the one place she knew she could sit and relax without anyone disturbing her.

Rana sat down in a chair by the window and looked out. The view was of the courtyard and a little bit of the city was visible over the gates. It was likely to be a busy day at the market because aside from the wind it was a beautiful spring day. Because the windows were just above the wall, it was impossible to see if Luce was still in the city or if he had gone through the gates by now.

Luce had told Rana all about his continuing quest to find magic in the world, especially since he now had the energy to help those who needed it. She had not suggested his quest was finished if the magic had come back to Proster, or Proster itself might need his help now that Hillel had taken the throne. Rana had thought about saying both and more but found instead she did not want to make him stay if he was determined to leave. If he did not love her enough to stay then she had no choice but to let him go.

Rana brushed away the tears starting to flow and tried to push all thoughts of Luce out of her mind. After all for him there probably had been many women who he had known, why should she think she was special? By his own admission, Luce had to be over a hundred years old, even though he barely looked to be in his twenties. He was handsome enough most women would be willing to spend time with him. Sure he gave off a strange energy, but that was likely because he used magic.

A whimper came from Rana's pocket. She looked

down to see Eustace's head popping out. He was her pet dragon, but due to lack of nutrients he had not grown beyond the length of Rana's hand. Eustace looked up at her with sadness in his silver eyes.

"I know," Rana said, "You'll miss him too." She scratched Eustace's neck and he nudged her wrist.

"But it is better this way," Rana said, "Because making him stay would just make everyone miserable. He is a wanderer with a mission; he does not need us trying to tie him down to one place. Besides, we can make it without him. I do not know how, but we will make it."

Eustace gave her a look suggesting he was not sure about that.

"We just have to figure out what to do about our situation," Rana said. Her gaze went back to the view out the window.

Eustace snuggled down into the pocket and snorted. Rana was not sure whether that was his opinion of the situation or his preference.

"I could accept my friend's, Daniella, offer to live with her family," Rana said, "They live in the city so I could remain close to the court. And they would not say anything about me having a baby out of wedlock to anyone unless they had my permission. But I would still be expected to make semi-regular appearances in court or to nearby nobles.

"There is the house Driscoll gave to Weldon and me in the city, but Weldon has been using it. He would never say anything bad about my presence there, but he likely wants to use it for his own family. And again I could not lock myself away from the world because it would be expected of me to make some appearances.

"Also, both would mean I am still close to the castle with Hillel on the throne. Despite Weldon's assurance that he can keep Hillel in line, I feel like the best thing to be is far out of Hillel's sphere of influence. I know he is king, which makes it difficult, but the closer physically to him we are the more likely we will end up in whatever trouble he is concocting."

Rana sighed as she looked out on the city. There was a feeling in the air suggesting the world would not be peaceful for very much longer; though Rana had not heard of any plans otherwise. In fact, Hillel had been a good king since he had been crowned in the fall. But then very little happens in Proster during the winter. With it being spring, Hillel was likely to start into whatever plans he had.

"Of course, there is the estate out in the country which came with the house in the city," Rana said.

Eustace's head popped back up out of the pocket and he looked up with interest.

"I would have to send some servants out to get it ready to be lived in and Weldon will likely demand I take some guards with me," Rana said, "But I would not have to make any appearances in court and no one would question my pregnancy without a husband. We would also be far away from Hillel and whatever he has planned."

Rana looked down at Eustace to find him nodding. She smiled for the first time all morning.

"Than that is our plan," Rana said, "We better hurry and get everything organized if we want to get out of here as soon as possible."

Rana stood up and Eustace withdrew back into the pocket. She turned to the door and was about to head out when something made her go to one of the shelves instead. Her hand reached out and picked up one of the books. It was The Prince and the Rogue by Thomas

Merritt. The book Luce had said he enjoyed, but Rana had not read. Rana took it with her as she left the library.

Rana had thought about going to her rooms but instead decided to go see Weldon. Since Hillel was not holding court and the lower court was closed for today, Weldon was not likely to be busy. His office was on the main floor beside the room where the lower court was held. Rana knocked on the door.

"Come in," Weldon's voice was muffled. Rana opened the door and stepped inside. There were three desks in the office, two closest to the door for clerks and Weldon's desk which was at the far end of the room. All three were piled high with paperwork, but the clerks were not in today. Weldon had not looked up from his work. Rana closed the door before taking one of the chairs and setting it in front of Weldon's desk. She sat down as he looked up.

"Good morning," Weldon said with a smile, "To what do I owe the privilege of your company today?"

"I have decided to move out to the country estate," Rana answered.

"But Driscoll requested you stay and help with advising his son," Weldon said, "I know you and Luce were close and his leaving hurt you, but there are others here who need you."

"I have thought it through," Rana said, "Hillel will never listen to me, no matter how much King Driscoll wanted him to and most of the other duties I was doing for King Driscoll have disappeared along with him. There is little for me to do in the city right now. Should that change I can move back, but I think right now the country estate is the best place for me to be."

"Are you sure?" Weldon asked.

"I am," Rana answered.

"The country estate needs work before anyone can live there," Weldon said.

"It will give me something to do while I find something to occupy my time," Rana said, "I will take my maid and see if I can hire some help from the nearby village. There is a couple who are currently taking care of the place. I will send them a message to let them know I am coming so they can prepare some rooms. Then all I have to do is pack my belongings and be off."

"I would suggest taking a couple guardsmen with you, at least until you are sure about the people from the village you are hiring," Weldon said, "For your own safety."

"Most of them are likely to be busy here," Rana said, "And I would not want to take them away from their duties."

"I will talk to Captain Kapena about it," Weldon said, "Even if there are no guards he can loan out, he will know good ones to hire."

"Okay," Rana said, "I was very much hoping to leave tomorrow morning."

"I will make sure the guards are ready when you are," Weldon said.

"I am going to miss you and Daniella," Rana said, "But this is better for me."

"It is not so far that letters are difficult to send either way," Weldon said, "And if you feel it is right for you than it most likely is, no matter my feelings on the subject. I would suggest you visit Daniella and tell her you are leaving rather than have her find out after you have left.

"I will talk to her sometime this afternoon," Rana said, "But first I need to make sure I have everything ready." Rana stood up.

"Very well," Weldon said.

"Thank you for being understanding," Rana said.

"As long as you are sure this is right," Weldon said.

"I am," Rana said before she left.

Rana went up to her rooms. Her maid had already cleaned and was not there. So Rana sat down at the desk in the sitting room. She wrote out the letter to the caretakers of the estate to let them know her plans. When she was finished, Rana sealed the letter and looked around. She would need to start packing immediately after lunch if she and her maid were going to get it all packed for tomorrow. Rana also had to contact her driver to get her carriage ready for the trip.

Rana figured she might as well do all that when she took the letter to the messenger because then she could talk to the castle steward and housekeeper at the same time. Then she would go for lunch. Her maid would be back after noon and Rana could have that conversation as well.

Eustace had left Rana's pocket when she had sat down at the desk to write the letter and was now sleeping in a patch of sunlight. Knowing Eustace, Rana figured he would sleep for several hours so she might as well leave him there and bring some food back for him.

Rana left him there and headed down to the area where the messengers spent their time. There were only three there. One was the older one who gave the jobs to the younger ones.

"How can I serve you, Lady Rana?" he asked.

"I need this letter taken to the Mungle Estate as soon as possible," Rana said.

"Of course," he said, "Barid can take it." He pointed to the older of the two messengers. Barid came over to them.

"He knows where to go and has a horse he can use to get there fast," the one said.

"Very well," Rana said, "Here is the letter and money for anything you need." Rana offered Barid both. He took them.

"I will get some lunch and then be on my way," Barid said.

"Good," Rana said. She left them and went in search of the castle steward.

She found the castle steward and the housekeeper talking in the entrance.

"Lady Rana," the castle steward said looking up at her, "What can we do for you today?"

"I wanted to let you know that I will be moving out to the Mungle Estate for a while," Rana said, "And I will be leaving tomorrow. I have already informed Weldon and sent a letter off to the caretakers of the estate. I will need food for the journey as well as another trunk for my belongings. My maid will be coming with me."

"I will let the kitchen staff know you need food," the castle steward said, "As well as tell Carter to get your carriage ready. Is there anything else?"

"I cannot think of anything else," Rana answered, "Thank you for letting Carter know."

"It is my pleasure," the castle steward said with a bow, "Your presence will be missed."

"By some," Rana said, "Oh, I just about forgot. Please send a message to Lady Daniella and let her know I will be stopping by this afternoon."

"I will do so," the castle steward said with a bow.

"What would you like done with your rooms?" the housekeeper asked.

"Close them up for the time being," Rana answered, "I will be back someday and will need them then."

"I will see to it tomorrow," the housekeeper said with a curtsy.

"Thank you both," Rana said.

"You are welcome," the castle steward said as both he and the housekeeper bowed. Rana smiled before heading off to the dining room for lunch.

After eating, Rana went back upstairs to her rooms. Her maid had not gotten back from lunch yet, but the castle steward had managed to get the trunk delivered.

Rana opened the lid and found it was clean, so she started to pack up her desk. She left the Thomas Merritt book where it was because she was going to pack it in the bag she would take with her in the carriage.

As Rana was finished packing up the desk her maid came back from lunch. The maid stopped in the doorway to stare at Rana rather than going about her work for the afternoon.

"We are leaving tomorrow," Rana said, "We are moving to the Mungle Estate for an indefinite period of time. We have to pack everything up today, but I also have to visit Daniella to tell her I am leaving."

"Yes, Lady Rana," the maid said.

"The housekeeper has said she would make sure the rooms would be closed up after we are gone," Rana said, "So just worry about packing things up."

"Yes, Lady Rana," the maid said.

Rana moved on to the next area she needed to pack up and her maid started to pack up the wardrobe.

It was getting late in the afternoon when Rana figured her maid could finish up and still have time to pack her own belongings. So Rana got washed up and dressed up. Then she left her maid and headed for the entrance to the castle. Her brother's carriage was waiting out front for her. The footman helped Rana up into the carriage before closing the door. And off the carriage went.

It did not take long for the carriage to reach Daniella's parent's house. Rana got out when the footman opened the door and helped her down. The butler was already opening the door. He waited as she went up the steps and inside before following her in.

"Lady Daniella is in the sitting room waiting for you," the butler said before heading in that direction. The Oakley family was considered middle nobility as their title was not very close to the royal family and they were not as wealthy as some. So their house was large and well-decorated but paled when compared to the castle. Rana, however, enjoyed her time here whenever she could visit.

The sitting room was the first doorway on the right and Daniella was seated waiting for Rana. When Rana followed the butler into the sitting room, Daniella got to her feet.

"Wonderful to see you," Daniella said coming over to hug Rana. The butler left them alone.

"It has not been forever since we last saw each other," Rana said when they let go and sat down.

"You have not been here since last week," Daniella said, "Which is the same thing." Daniella poured them each a cup of tea before handing one cup to Rana and taking the other for herself.

"How has your week been?" Rana asked, "Did Rook ask for your hand as you thought he would?"

"We are definitely behind in news," Daniella said, "Rook was caught in bed with his sister's handmaiden by his mother and the handmaiden is claiming a swollen belly. Who could blame her when she has already been seen in such a position with him and it could gain her a much better position? My father told me I could no longer see Rook as his reputation was ruined and he wanted a better pairing for me."

"How do you feel about it?" Rana asked.

"Disappointed," Daniella answered, "I am starting to get too old for a really good pairing and there are fewer men to choose from. I want to be married with a household of my own and the possibility is starting to drift away from me. Rook was far from perfect, but he seemed to be getting ready to ask for my hand. Do you not worry about ending up an old maid?"

"Not really," Rana answered, "I was always taught that the right one will come along when the time is right. So there was never pressure to find the right man in a certain amount of time."

"But your lover is going to ask for your hand, right?" Daniella asked.

"No, he left this morning to continue his quest," Rana answered, "As far as I know he is not coming back."

"What about you?" Daniella asked, "Did you not ask him to stay?"

"I could not," Rana answered, "I could not ask him to stay when I knew he would not be happy staying here. He needs the space the road provides for him."

"What are you going to do now?" Daniella asked.

"I am going to the Mungle Estate for a while," Rana answered.

"Why?" Daniella clasped Rana's hand as if Rana was going to disappear if she let go.

"Because I sense trouble coming to court," Rana answered, "And I do not wish to cause my family any scandal."

"How could there be a scandal?" Daniella asked, "You have never done anything that would cause trouble."

"My lover left me something that will cause the

scandal," Rana said, "But he left before I could tell him about it and I have no way to send a letter to him."

"You said you were only going for a while," Daniella said, "What are you going to do once the child is born?"

"Raise the child," Rana said, "I am not likely to be back as long as Hillel is on the throne and scheming away."

"What if your lover returns?" Daniella asked.

"Then I hope Weldon lets him know where I am," Rana said, "I decided to come over today and tell you what I was doing because I am leaving tomorrow. I made the decision to leave this morning and I believe it is best if I go as soon as possible."

"I am going to miss you," Daniella said.

"And I will miss you," Rana said, "I wish you the best of luck in finding a husband who is right for you. I will write as often as there is news and you can send letters to me. You do not even have to pay a messenger, all you have to do is take them to the castle and give them to Weldon. He will make sure they get to me."

"I will do that," Daniella said, "But it will hardly be the same as you coming for tea on a regular basis."

"I know," Rana said, "I am going to miss it. I probably will not be out there more than a week before I miss all the gossip from the court, but it will be better for me out there."

"If you say so," Daniella said, "But I am going to miss you being here very much. Though if I end up an old maid I might go out there and join you."

"Write before you come and I will make sure there is a room prepared," Rana said.

Daniella wrapped her arms around Rana and held her tight as if she was scared to let go. Rana hugged her back while trying to hold the tears in. Daniella was not successful in that as Rana could see when they finally let go of each other.

"I should get back before supper is served," Rana said, "And I will leave tomorrow morning. I will miss you and I will write as soon as I arrive at the estate.'

"Okay," Daniella said wiping the tears from her face. Rana and Daniella both got to their feet. They hugged again with more tears running down Daniella's face.

Rana left the room before her own tears could start. The butler arrived at that moment to show her out. The carriage had not moved, so Rana was helped in immediately by the footman. The door closed behind her. Rana looked between the half open curtains at her best friend's house and felt the wetness of tears on her own face though she had not given them permission to fall.

When the carriage reached the court yard, Rana wiped off her face with a handkerchief and hoped her face was not too red that people would notice she had been crying. Once the carriage stopped the footman opened the door and helped her out. Rana went into the castle and headed for the dining room. She did not reach it before the castle steward found her.

"Lady Rana," the castle steward said, "May I have a moment of your time?"

"Certainly," Rana said as she stopped, "What is it?"

"I talked to the cook," the castle steward said, "There will be breakfast waiting for you whenever you get up. Also, there will be enough food sent with you to last the trip."

"Thank you," Rana said.

"I spoke with Carter and he has everything ready for tomorrow," the castle steward said.

"That is good," Rana said.

"I also talked to Weldon," the castle steward said,

"And Captain Kapena had suggested you take Duard and Havard with you. They are still good at their jobs, but they are both a month from the end of their employment with the royal guard. Once that month is up, if you wish to keep them around you will have to hire them on privately."

"A lot can happen in a month," Rana said, "Best to deal with that closer to the time. Meanwhile, it will be good to have guards."

"I found another trunk for your maid to put her belongings into," the castle steward said, "As well as got some of your trunks already loaded into the carriage, so tomorrow there will be less work before you can leave."

"Thank you very much," Rana said, "I appreciate everything you have done for me." Rana kissed the castle steward on the cheek. His face went red as she headed for the dining room.

During supper, Rana slipped some scraps into her pocket because she knew Eustace would be hungry by now, if he were not to upset with her for disappearing on him. When supper was over, Rana went up to her rooms. She found Eustace sitting on the desk looking around as if he had lost something. Rana sat down in the chair and he looked up at her with interest.

"I brought some scraps from supper," Rana said taking them out and putting them on the desk, "But it is not much."

Eustace dove into them as if they were the finest feast he had ever laid eyes on.

"Everything is ready for us to leave in the morning," Rana said, "Everything is packed, the carriage is ready, there will be food, and I said goodbye to Daniella. Tomorrow morning I will say goodbye to Weldon and then we will be off.

"Daniella asked about Luce coming back and whether I had made any plans to let him know where I am, but I do not think he will be coming back. Or if he does come back it will likely be some time after I am dead and gone."

Eustace pulled his head out of the pile of scraps to look at her. He cocked his head and squinted in confusion.

"Luce claimed he first visited Proster when Hillel's grandfather was a young king," Rana said, "That makes over a hundred years between visits. If he keeps up that pattern, I am not going to see him again, but our child might be lucky and get to."

Eustace stared her a moment longer before going back to his food. Sometimes Rana wished he could talk. Luce had explained that Eustace was a young dragon and as such did not yet have the ability. It took a few hundred years for a dragon to be considered an adult and develop verbal skills. Luce also said Eustace's growth was stunted due to lack of food during an crucial growth period, however, should Eustace reach another growth period and had food available to him he might get bigger. But he would not get to the size of an average dragon his age.

Rana was not sure whether to be happy about that or not. If he did not get any bigger, she would have a great pet for the rest of her life. But if Eustace did get bigger than he could go out on his own and not have to be a pet at all. It was a difference in having freedom or not and she thought he deserved a chance to be free.

Rana's maid came in and Rana looked up at her.

"Everything has been packed, Lady Rana," her maid said.

"Good," Rana replied, "We should get to bed early so we can get started at dawn."

"Yes, Lady Rana," the maid said.

Rana left Eustace eating and got into her nightdress with her maid's help. Rana climbed into bed while her maid closed the curtains and prepared the room for the night. Then the maid went to her own room and closed the door. Rana laid there and waited to drift off to sleep.

She was starting to drift off when she felt Eustace land on the pillow beside her and curl up in a ball. Once he was comfortable, Rana fell asleep.

A knocking sound caused Rana to open her eyes and sit up. It was dark in the room so Rana could not see much. There was no second knock. Rana listened carefully for any other noises that might suggest she was in danger. Though Eustace must have still been asleep so whatever made the noise was not likely to be a danger to her.

A muffled screech made Rana freeze and hold her breath as she tried to figure out where the sounds were coming from. She finally realized it had come from her maid's room.

Rana thought about getting up to check it out, but she did not have a weapon on, or near her. She could probably find a guard in the hallway to help out, but she would have to be soundless about moving.

Before Rana could move, she heard a moan coming from the room, but it did not sound like someone in need of help. It sounded like someone who would not want to be disturbed. There was a second person making noise. One sounded like Rana's maid and the other like the carriage driver, Carter.

Rana lay back down. She closed her eyes and put the pillow over her ears so she could sleep in peace.

STARTING OF THE TRIP AND THE BEGINNING OF THE NOVEL

Rana woke up before the sun had risen and got out of bed. She dressed herself this morning before finishing what little packing could not be done the night before. By the time Rana was finished, her maid had woken up and dressed. Rana sent her off to get the men to move the last trunks and get breakfast.

Eustace did not move until the sun rose, at which point Rana's maid arrived with the breakfast tray. Rana, her maid, and Eustace sat down to eat while the men took away the trunks.

When they were finished eating, Rana did a quick check to make sure everything had been packed. Then she put Eustace in her pocket before her and her maid went down to the entrance way.

The spring morning was cold so everyone was waiting there to say goodbye. There was Weldon, the castle steward, the housekeeper, the cook, and Hillel's wife,

Arabella. Rana hugged her brother.

"I will miss you," Weldon said, "And I am sure Driscoll would not want you to go, but I understand your reasons for leaving."

"I will miss you, too," Rana said before she let go.

The castle steward, the housekeeper, and the cook bowed. The cook gave the package with the food to Rana's maid as they went passed him. Rana stopped in front of Arabella. Arabella was about medium height and average weight. Her blonde hair was long and braided before being wrapped around her head a few times. The green eyes had a trace of sadness and innocence. Her green dress fit her well, but she did not appear to be wearing a corseted bodice under it. Also, Arabella had a glow similar to one Rana had seen in her own face recently. Until yesterday morning, Rana had thought it was love. But at least, Arabella was married and there would be no trace of scandal around her child. Rana hoped for the best for Arabella.

"I am sorry you are leaving," Arabella said, "It was an honour to meet and get to know you."

"It is the same for me," Rana said, "And I wish good luck and fortune in your life."

"You will be missed here at the castle," Arabella said with a sad smile. Rana wrapped her arms around Arabella and pulled her close. Arabella hugged her back. After a moment they separated. Rana turned to wave to everyone else before going out the door.

The carriage was all packed up and waiting in front of the main doors. There were two guards on horses nearby. The one guard from beside the door opened the carriage door and held it while the second guard helped Rana and her maid inside. Once both of them were comfortable, the guard closed the door, and the carriage started moving.

Rana watched as they left the courtyard, went down through the city, and finally out the city gates. Only once she could no longer see the city did Rana dig into her bag for something to do. She took out the Thomas Merritt novel and flipped through the pages until she arrived at the first page of the story. Then Rana started to read.

Prince Kenneth was mesmerized by the delicate wings and vibrant tones of the lady in the humming bird costume, he could not remember the like of it at any of the yearly masquerade balls that his father, King Drax, held to mark the end of summer. His own costume of a bear's skin was a total mismatch for the fine feathers of his new obsession but that bothered him not at all for he knew underneath it beat the heart of the prince of this realm. The brief consideration of his own place in things brought him to question hers.

As the guests arrived, Prince Kenneth had taken not a little pride in the fact that he believed that he could name everyone who came through the door by the habitual gaits, off hand gestures and distinctive voices that were so familiar from court except the hummingbird. She was an enigma. Since it was demanded that he keep a close eye on what happened in court, Prince Kenneth was certain that no foreign princess, or countess or even lady of enough consequence to receive an invitation was visiting. Which meant she was there without invitation, a definite breach of security. All of which made Kenneth desire to meet her, that and she danced so divinely, that was if he could just brush away the gnat that was Lord Brawn. Perhaps the man's costume was closer to right, a billy goat, to stubborn to accept that his company was looking elsewhere while he held forth on nothing more than how this year's annual ball was the best one he had attended. The hummingbird's quick movements were leading her to the far end of the room and a quick glance let him know that he was not the only man watching her.

Good manners forbade Prince Kenneth from cutting the man in front of him, because at exactly midnight the masks would come off and his father would hear about the slight. Frustration at the conventions of court and his own place in it rose up in Prince Kenneth, his whole life was bound up in rules and customs, he looked back at the hummingbird.

Just then his cousin, Reginald, Duke of, for the moment Prince Kenneth could not remember as his vision grew red, offered the hummingbird a dance. Since he had not yet made the lady's acquaintance he could make no claim to jealously but it was there just the same and he was not going to lose sight of her while she might fall under the spell of that rascal.

Although the duke was dressed as a stallion, Prince Kenneth thought a jackass might have been a more appropriate choice. He only hoped the hummingbird would discover that for herself before the dance was finished.

A pirate, who Prince Kenneth easily identified as Lord Hayes, paused to slip a comment into Lord Brawn's soliloquy and was somehow sucked into the vortex of Lord Brawn. It proved just the opportunity Prince Kenneth needed to step back out of the conversation. He felt a moments pang at abandoning Lord Hayes but it was either that or snub Brawn in a way that could cause the kind of bad feelings that his father warned him led to treason and sedition.

The dance was ending when Prince Kenneth located the couple and he could see Duke Reginald was making a plea for another dance. It was the kind of offer that lead places as second dances were reserved for someone more than just a new acquaintance. Prince Kenneth got a slight thrill when it became evident that the hummingbird was wise enough to deny the request. Prince Kenneth could tell by the manner of his leaving that his cousin was neither happy nor proud of her answer. Lady Bella twittered at him. The hummingbird hear the first note of the next song and turned to see who else was there.

Prince Kenneth approached her side. "You seem eager to dance, do you wish a new partner? May I offer myself?"

The hummingbird turned and looked him up and down then she said with a soft voice and a curtsy. "That would be lovely."

Prince Kenneth lifted her hand in his and placed his hand at her waist. He looked into her eyes as he swept her into the steps of the waltz. There was a twinkle behind the emerald green eyes. Aside from her eyes which held him only her lips were visible. Soft pink lips with none of the artificial colouring that tasted bad as some ladies used. What little of her hair he could see was the hue of toffee, one of his favorite treats. He was tempted to tighten his hold on her to see what other charms he would uncover. Still if she sent Duke Reginald away that indicated that she was not here to find a bed partner for the night. For Prince Kenneth had little doubt as to the suggestion that got the duke summary dismissed. Instead Prince Kenneth choose to use politeness.

"Has the king's party amused you?" Prince Kenneth asked.

"I have never seen anything quite like it and yes, it amuses me," the hummingbird answered, "Although one thing has me stumped."

"Really what is that?"

"How do you know who is who?"

"Mostly it is a matter of knowing the mannerisms of the individuals." Prince Kenneth smiles. "Believe I could guess all but one of the guests without hesitation."

"Really?" the emerald eyes sparkled, "Even me?"

"You retain your mystery for now," Prince Kenneth replied, "Would it upset you to know that you just sent off a duke who is second in line for the throne?"

"He was crude and not at all amusing, really he was a duke! Wait this this why you requested this dance?" the hummingbird frowns, "To undercover my identity?"

"At a masked ball, it is part of the game, to guess the names of one's fellow guests," Prince Kenneth answers. "So would it not be unheard of to ask for such a reason."

"*There are many better reasons to ask a woman to dance,*" *the hummingbird answered.*

"*I agree,*" *Prince Kenneth said,* "*But the manner in which you sent the duke off suggested to me that trotting them out might leave me mid-floor without a partner.*"

"*It was the man himself I rejected, not all men. As I said he was crude.*" *the hummingbird replied.*

"*Not a popular sentiment among many ladies,*" *Prince Kenneth said,* "*Which makes you in my estimation a rare jewel.*"

"*Hardly that, just one with particular tastes,*" *the hummingbird said,* "*Am I giving you any clues?*"

The last notes of the song slowed to signal its approaching end.

"*I think I need a few more hints,*" *Prince Kenneth said,* "*Another dance to learn a little more?*"

"*And risk being unmasked?*" *the hummingbird smiled,* "*On the other hand you are far more amusing that the duke so perhaps it will be to my benefit.*"

"*I thank you for the favour,*" *Prince Kenneth said. He broke off the last movement of the dance to take her hand and kiss it. Laughter filled those emerald eyes. They remained touching after the song ended and as the musicians got ready to play the next one. It did not take long as many of the dancers changed.*

"*Has anyone guessed who you are?*" *the hummingbird asked as the music started.*

"*None have attempted tonight,*" *Prince Kenneth answered,* "*Once your mask is gone the entertainment goes out of the evening and the king extracts a penalty for incorrect guesses so no one wishes to be wrong.*"

"*Could you not ignore the guess and continue wearing the mask?*"

"*That would be against the rules and you would not get an invitation to next year's ball.*"

"*But still, you could break the rules. Would you?*" *the emerald eyes were curious, but she gave no clues as to whether she wanted him to be a rule keeper or a breaker.*

"It hardly matters, it is rare that anyone guesses at my identity. I usually have very good costumes, so I have never been tempted to break the rules."

"You believe you know everyone?" the hummingbird asked, "Yet none have lost their masks."

"Just because I know does not mean I make public guesses," Prince Kenneth replied, "The more people without masks the easier it is to guess those who still wear one."

"So you bend the rules," the emerald eyes still sparkle but only to reflect the light of the candles so Prince Kenneth remained unclear on how to proceed. The only thing he knew for certain was that she was not a member of the court for he was certain few of the guests did not know who he is. He needed to find out more about her.

"Now you." Prince Kenneth says, "Do you prefer to break the rule or enforce it?"

"I like to break rules," the hummingbird answered, "I like the element of fun in it. Does that help you figure out who I am?"

"Not yet," Prince Kenneth answered, "But I have a few minutes to figure it out."

The emerald eyes laugh, yet Prince Kenneth smiled because he cared little about her identity and more about enjoying this dance. He saw no reason to rush its end.

"If a duke is not good enough for you," Prince Kenneth said, "What do you look for in a dance partner?"

"The ability to hold an intelligent conversation while dancing," the hummingbird answered, "with the humility to listen to their partner as a fellow human being rather than just talking about themselves. Also someone with a sense of humour."

"Have I any hope?" Prince Kenneth asked.

"More so than the duke did," the hummingbird answered, "Add to that you are a skilled dancer. It is your reason for asking me to dance that is causing me concern."

"Would it help if I admitted that I had also considered asking

for a dance in the garden?" Prince Kenneth asked, "We could find a quiet spot to waltz without interruption."

"And what awaits us in the garden?" the hummingbird asked.

"The king is extremely proud of his gardens," Prince Kenneth said, "He collects rare plants and this time of the year it is both interesting and, for a week or so yet, warm enough to stroll comfortably without a coat."

"And if I said yes, we would go there?" She asks.

"It would be best to wait until the end of the dance before we walk away." Prince Kenneth smiles. "That way people would assume we are going for refreshments."

"Will we not attract undo attention, a bear and hummingbird together?" the hummingbird asked.

"Ours are not the most outlandish costumes," Prince Kenneth answered, "You will find that after a few glasses of wine are consumed, the guests will lose some of their inhibitions especially while they were disguised."

"The dance is ending," the hummingbird said.

"A few more minutes," Prince Kenneth said, "Let us enjoy it."

Their eyes hold each other while their feet complete the steps of the dance. When the final note of the song faded away, some of the dancers left the floor and were replaced with other. Prince Kenneth held the hummingbird's hand as he guided her off the floor. He was very observant of the crowd as he guided her. He did not wish to meet those who would try to strike up a conversation with him, yet he did not draw attention with speed or impoliteness as might cause suspicion about their purpose. A single person stopping them might cause enough of a delay that the party would encroach on his plans for privacy.

The still sober crowd was engaged in one of two pursuits, dancing or standing around watching the dancing and conversing in groups. A few who paid attention to who left the ball gave little attention to a bear and hummingbird wandering towards the refreshment table. And those people who did probably thought that the dancers were merely searching for a drink before returning to the floor. Prince Kenneth used that to his advantage to slip out the door the servants used to bring in food and drink.

Since the food and drink had been newly laid out none of the servants were in the hall and there were no guards were posted here. The hummingbird slowed for a minute anyway to check, but Prince Kenneth was not worried about it. He kept a hold of her hand and walked a little faster. Now that there was no one to stop them, he did not feel the need to stay at the same pace.

The hummingbird joined him at that speed. Prince Kenneth looked over at her and found her smiling. He felt the sense of freedom go through him that always went through him when he did something he was not supposed to do for he had been instructed to stay at the ball until the unveiling.

"Come on," Prince Kenneth whispered, "This way." He tugged on her hand as he started to run. She let out a quiet laugh and then ran with him. Their foot falls rang down the hall, but there is no one to hear or complain.

They ran down that hallway and the one on the right at the end of it. Finally they reached the door and slipped through it. Prince Kenneth closed it behind them. They stopped on the other side to catch their breaths and laugh.

The doorway lead into an alcove of bushes that hid them from view unless a person was specifically looking. They could see the high bushes that surrounded the walking paths, but little else except that path from the alcove into the maze like area. Once they had caught their breath, Prince Kenneth helped her down the step and along the stone path. The hummingbird looked around in interest at the various bushes and flowers as well as the bright moon and stars.

"This is better than you described," the hummingbird's voice was low and hushed. Prince Kenneth could have pointed out that all of the court had been out here at some point, or that visiting nobles would likely have seen a garden similar to this one, but he kept quiet and just enjoyed being out here with her. Most of the woman *in court were boring, married, or pushy and this lady did not seem to be any of those. So Prince Kenneth decided he did not need to know who she was, just that he liked her company.*

"I am glad you like it," Prince Kenneth said. He let the hummingbird go ahead of him as she was flitted from flower to flower and paid no attention to him.

They traveled the path as it twisted and turned with smaller plants in front of middle sized bushes and then hedge behind it. It was impossible to see over them to tell if just how alone they were. There was just the rustle of the wind, the chirping of insects, their footsteps on the path and her sounds as she appreciated the beauty of the plants. The perfume of flowers swept in from other parts of the gardens and the moon provided all the light necessary to see. Soft rays shone down on the hummingbird and made her sparkle. The glitter on her costume and skin made her mesmerizing to watch as she practically dance along the path.

Prince Kenneth barely remembered to keep up with her, he was absorbed just watching her. She got so far ahead that she was almost around a corner from him, Prince Kenneth sped up to catch up but stopped when she suddenly looked straight at him.

He could not miss the message in those eyes this time, the green was shadowed by the quality of the moonlight but the intensity of the emotion shone through and the answer came from deep within himself. Later he might question how much the influences of the moon, stars and atmosphere of garden played a part in his fall but never would he doubt that this woman would reside without competition within the confines of his heart and even his father's kingdom would not be too much to pay for the privilege of loving her.

Without another thought, Prince Kenneth lifted his mask from his face to the top of his head. The hummingbird did the same. Her skin was slightly tanned and her face thinner than what was popular at court. All her features were the right size for her face and her lips looked especially kissable. Prince Kenneth took a step toward her with that intent in mind. She flashed him an slight smile and then took off running.

Prince Kenneth hesitated for only a second as her action caught him off guard but then he ran after her. Like her costume suggested she moved quickly, dodging back and forth, she teased him by stopping to hide just out of sight then popping up when he thought she had fled or squeezing down beside a bush only to run the other direction just as he passed. At one point he grasp her hand, only to have her wiggle free but then she giggled. After that he never really lost her again for all he had to do was to listen for the giggle.

In the end catching was simple, Prince Kenneth simply slipped up behind her as she stood staring at the peach hued roses which graced the garden in the center of the maze. The garden was a large square with stone paths between the beds and benches for people to sit on while they looked at the roses.

"They are the most beautiful things I have ever seen." She said as he pulled her against him.

"I disagree, you are the lovelier than any rose." He leaned down to speak directly into her ear. She sunk into his chest to rest. Once she had her breath back, he took it away simply by turning her around to kiss her as Prince Kenneth had been longing to do since he had set eyes on her. Her arms slipped around his neck. He put one hand behind her neck and the other on her lower back to draw her closer to him. Her lips were soft and she smelled like lavender. Prince Kenneth never wanted to let the kiss end, but he finally did.

He looked down into those emerald eyes and saw the same longing which had taken over his whole being. He no longer was anything without her. And all he wanted to do was possess her. He kissed her again and she melted into him. If it was not for their costumes, Prince Kenneth felt they would melded together.

The sound of voices came over the bushes to them from the direction of the palace. Both Prince Kenneth and the hummingbird jumped apart a little bit and looked toward the noise. She turned to him with a look that suggested it might not be a good idea to get caught kissing in the rose garden. Prince Kenneth knew better than to get caught kissing in the rose garden. Since the rest of the guest were now coming into the garden he had to think of another place to take her.

Prince Kenneth tucked her hand into his elbow and escorted her around the roses to the exit from the other side of the maze. Guests walking in the gardens during the night rarely ventured passed the rose garden. Prince Kenneth and the hummingbird reached the path and started to run to get away from the people. They did not stop until they reached the another entrance into the maze. This entrance brought them into the orchard. The first several rows of trees were for peaches and had been stripped bare a month ago.

The hummingbird did not let go of Prince Kenneth's hand but started forward into the orchard. There was plenty of space for the moonlight to come through to create fascinating patterns on the ground. Prince Kenneth pulled the hummingbird to him, but instead of kissing her, he started to dance. She followed his lead as they wound their way through the peach trees and the rows of pear trees that followed.

When they reached the rows of apples trees, they stopped. The peaches and pears had been cleaned off the trees, but the apples were set to be picked later that week. Prince Kenneth and the hummingbird took a break from their dancing to just walk together.

The hummingbird reached up and picked a low hanging apple. She took a bite out of it before offering it to Prince Kenneth. He accepted it and had a bite before passing it back. They ate as they wandered through a few rows of apples trees. There were twice as many rows of apple trees as there was peach and pear trees.

There were still several more rows of apple trees when Prince Kenneth stopped and threw away the apple core. The hummingbird stopped to look at him. He pulled her to him and kissed her lips with soft feathery kisses. He kissed down to her jaw and along it to her neck. She gripped his jaw to lead his lips back to her mouth and deepened the kiss. His hands wandered down her body and *back up. She removed his mask completely from his head and dropped it nearby so that she could run her fingers through his hair. Her mask came off and was dropped near his. He started to unhook the back of her dress. When he got to its bottom, she shimmied out of it and let it drop to the ground. His costume joined it shortly after. They used his bear costume as bedding as they laid down under an apple tree and made love.*

When the temperature dropped enough to cause goose bumps, Prince Kenneth helped her back into her dress. The ball was concluded and everyone had retired to their rooms when the couple returned into the palace. Prince Kenneth skirted the main doors to avoid meeting any guards as he took her back to his room. Once inside they climbed into his bed, where they made love until they fell into an exhausted sleep.

Rana put her finger in her place in the book and looked out the window. The sounds of people had interrupted her reading. The carriage was passing through the town of Laurie and was currently going through the marketplace, which was busy this day. It was slow going because of all the other people and the closeness of the stalls. Carter was working hard to avoid hitting anyone.

The carriage kept showing further and further down the closer they got to the centre of the market. At the centre square, the carriage was closer to stopped than moving. An older woman noticed Rana looking out the window and came over to the carriage. She did not have any goods to peddle.

"Would ye lady wish to have ye fortune told?" the old woman asked in a creaky voice, "Won't take more than a minute or two." The old woman held out her wrinkled hands.

"No, thank you," Rana answered keeping her hands

inside the carriage despite the pull to let the old woman take them.

The old woman was just about to say something else when Eustace stuck his head out the window and hissed at her. The old woman's eyes went red and she backed off. She was quickly lost in the crowd. Eustace stayed where he was for another minute as the carriage inched forward. Finally, Eustace relaxed and went back into the pocket.

Rana's hands shook for a few minutes until she assured herself that Eustace would not have gone back if she was still in danger from the witch. A chill did settle in on her as Rana realized what she had seen. She would have to send a letter of warning to Weldon about magical beings in Proster as well as keeping Eustace close by for protection. Rana was glad she had the guards with her, even if they had no idea what to do about anything magical.

The carriage started moving faster as it got a little further along the road. Rana kept looking out the window to see if the witch followed them until they were going much faster and leaving the market behind them. She never saw a trace of the witch. When she was sure the witch was gone, Rana opened the book to where she left off and started to read.

Prince Kenneth was much more alert when the village finally came in sight. It had been a quiet and enjoyable three days without any thought of what was going on back at the palace. The village itself was about half the size of the palace grounds with a low wall all the way around it. There were some pastures outside the wall, but no buildings. It was the middle of the afternoon, so everyone was out and about. The villagers all stopped and stared at Prince Kenneth and his party as they went passed. The adults of the village called their good days, but the children just stood and watched. Occasionally a child would follow for a short ways.

Prince Kenneth paid attention to the people around him as they went along the road through the village. Most of the adults wore homespun in browns, blues, or greys; the men in trousers and shirts and the woman in dresses. The children were in all sorts of clothing, but mostly dirty from playing outside. None of the faces stood out and Prince Kenneth did not think he would remember any of them later.

Then he saw a little girl standing in front a tailor's shop with other children and she stared at him. The girl had long, unbound brown curls which reminded Prince Kenneth of the mess of hair he saw when he looked in the mirror, but her eyes matched those of the hummingbird who disappeared six years ago. The lips and nose also looked like those of the hummingbird. The girl herself appeared to be between five and six.

Prince Kenneth wanted to rein in his horse and steal her back to the palace, but he feared the villagers would try to stop him. She may have parents around who would miss her. Or the hummingbird may live here and he could find her again. His love could have married and the girl could think someone else was her father. Prince Kenneth was not sure he could handle seeing the hummingbird married to another man. He would never ask her to leave her husband, or do anything else that he would love to do to and with her again.

Prince Kenneth's group moved along and the girl stayed where she was, which meant she was out of sight in a few minutes. He searched the faces they passed more carefully this time, in hopes that one of them might be his hummingbird. But they reached their destination without any sign of her.

The largest house in the village was the manor house. It was several stories tall with a garden in the front and what looked to be a stable in the back. The house was made from bricks with actual glass in the windows rather than just shutters. The man they came to see was already outside waiting for them. He likely received word of their arrival shortly after they were sighted. Prince Kenneth got down from his horse and went over to his father's friend.

"Lord Sterling," Prince Kenneth said with a slight nod of his head.

"Welcome, Prince Kenneth," Lord Sterling did a proper bow in greeting, "Your men can take the horses to the stable around back."

Prince Kenneth glanced at the guards and nodded. Lord Jegger had already gotten down from his own horse and was joining Prince Kenneth and Lord Sterling. The guards took all the horses and headed for the back of the house. Lord Sterling led the way inside. Prince Kenneth and Lord Jegger followed him through the hall to a sitting room. Lord Sterling gestured for them to take a seat before pouring them each a drink and joining them.

"To what do I owe this honour?" Lord Sterling asked once Prince Kenneth and Lord Jegger had a drink in hand and were settled.

"My father requested your presence at court," Prince Kenneth answered.

"Is there trouble?" Lord Sterling asked.

"There are rumblings of something vague," Prince Kenneth answered, "which we have not been able to track to a source."

"Your father must be worried about it happening soon if he is sending you here now," Lord Sterling said, "Is anything likely to happen while you are gone?"

"He does not believe so," Prince Kenneth answered, "But again there are only signs and no direct action against him."

"I will go to court at his request," Lord Sterling said, "If he is troubled than that is my place. However, I will need a little time to make sure everything will be okay here in my absence."

"How long?" Prince Kenneth asked.

"A day or two," Lord Sterling answered.

"That will be fine," Prince Kenneth replied.

"There will be little for you to do in that time," Lord Sterling

said, "This village is quiet and has very few troubles."

"Actually, I was wondering about one of the children we saw," Prince Kenneth said.

"Which one?" Lord Sterling asked.

"A little girl," Prince Kenneth answered, "About five or six. Long, brown, curly hair. Emerald eyes. Just under four feet tall and skinny."

"That sounds like the widow's charge," Lord Sterling said.

"Widow?" Prince Kenneth asked.

"Aileen once was married to one of my vassals but at his death she moved out of the village. She has a house at the far side of the field near the edge of the forest there," Lord Sterling answered, "She comes into the village every couple of days to sell her goods. She brings the girl with her. The girl is not hers, but no one has seen the mother. The mother may have stayed with the widow for a while after the girl's birth, but no one know for certain. If she did, she is gone now. The girl appears happy and well cared for, so no one interferes in the matter. Why does the matter interest you?"

"The girl looks like a woman I met six years back," Prince Kenneth answered, "She went missing shortly afterwards."

"Well, if the girl is in the village then the widow will be," Lord Sterling said, "I can send a request for her to come talk to you."

"I would much appreciate that," Prince Kenneth said.

"Then if you will excuse me, I will go do that," Lord Sterling said as he stood up, "As well as start to get ready to leave."

"You are excused," Prince Kenneth said. Lord Sterling bowed and left the room. Prince Kenneth looked over at Lord Jegger and found the man had fallen asleep. Shaking his head at the lord, Prince Kenneth took out the papers his father had sent with him.

The carriage stopped, and Rana looked out the window to see they were at an inn. Carter was getting down from the driver's seat, and a man was coming out of the inn to greet him. The inn was in good condition, and likely cost more than the average person could afford. It was painted a dark red with white trim. There were three windows in the top storey of the same size. The lower level had a window about the same size as the ones above on the right side and a larger one of the left side. The larger one probably had the main room behind it.

Carter and the man talked for a moment before Carter came to the door of the carriage and opened it. Rana was helped out first before her maid was.

"They are getting the rooms ready," Carter said, "In the meantime, supper is in the main room for you."

"Thank you," Rana said before heading into the inn. Her maid gathered what luggage Rana would need for the night before Carter took the carriage around to the back of the inn where the stable was.

Inside was decorated in more reds with white trim. The main room had several tables scattered in carefully placed intervals. Each table had four chairs placed around it and the chairs were made for the comfort of the guests. A couple was sitting at a table eating. They looked up at her before going back to their own conversation. Both wore clothing of high quality, but not as expensive as Rana's own dress.

To one side of the main room was a door with a staircase next to it. The wall across from the entrance was a doorway that likely led to the kitchen. The smell from the kitchen was enough for Rana to find a table near the window. Supper was brought to her by a large woman in a food splattered apron over a brown dress and a smile. Rana smiled in return as she was given a plate of food and a cup of cider. The roasted meat, potatoes, and chunk of bread all looked so good. Rana barely waited for the woman to leave her before starting to eat.

The sun had been getting closer to the horizon when Carter had stopped the carriage. While Rana was eating it gave off its final brightness before sinking behind the far mountains. The sky went dark and a young man walked around the room lighting candles for the few customers at the inn. A fire was built in the fireplace to warm the room from the chill that came with the darkness.

Rana finished eating and took her book back out to continue reading for a few minutes before she would go up to her room for the night.

It was late afternoon when the butler entered the sitting room. Lord Jegger had been provided a bed and Lord Sterling was busy. Prince Kenneth looked up at the butler.

"Yes?" Prince Kenneth said.

"The widow is here to see you," the butler replied.

"Send her in," Prince Kenneth said pushing the papers he had been reading aside.

"Yes, sir," the butler said before withdrawing.

A few minutes later, he escorted a woman into the room. The woman was at the later end of middle age. Her hair was black with grey streaks through it and her brown eyes were clear. She held herself straight and her lined face showed more worry than laughter. Prince Kenneth had stood on her arrival.

"I am Prince Kenneth," Prince Kenneth said, "I appreciate you coming to talk to me. Please have a seat."

The woman sat down across from him, but did not relax. He sat back down as the butler left the room.

"Your name?" Prince Kenneth asked.

"Aileen," the woman answered.

"And the name of your charge?" Prince Kenneth asked.

"What does she have to do with this?" Aileen asked.

"She is the reason I wanted to talk to you," Prince Kenneth answered, "I saw her today as I was riding in and I recognized

her."

"That child has never been out of this village," Aileen said, "It would be impossible for you to recognize her."

"She looks like her mother," Prince Kenneth said, "A woman I met six years ago at the masquerade ball. She disappeared shortly after that and I have been trying to find her. I have reason to wanting to know about any child she bore."

"The child's name is Isadora," Aileen said, "And I am the only parent she has ever known. Her mother did not stay."

"Tell me the story?" Prince Kenneth asked.

"I suppose," Aileen answered, "It is not a secret. She stumbled out of the woods one evening. The clouds had been gathering all day and it was a heavy calm which meant the storm was coming. I do not know where she came from or why she had not found a place to stay before this village. She was in birthing pains when she knocked on my door. She begged for shelter and for help with the child. It was her first child and she did not know what to do. My mother was a trained mid-wife, so I had knowledge to help her and could not turn away anyone with such need.

"As the birthing pains got worse, so did the storm. The child came into the world as the storm reached its height, which if I were a superstitious nature I would think the events were connected and that the child was a bad omen. But I am not and the child has shown no signs of evil tendencies.

"She named the child Isadora and loved her. She stayed to nurse the child, but left when the child was old enough to do without her mother's milk. I have not seen the mother since that time. If she visits she does not come to the door or into the house. I have been taking care of the child the best I know how. You believe you are the father?"

"It is possible," Prince Kenneth answered, "But I do not know enough about the actions of the child's mother to know if there are any other possibilities."

"From her responses to my questions of the father, I gathered

that there was only one possibility," Aileen said, "And if that is you then the child belongs with a blood relation over a stranger to the family. She will not be ready to go until tomorrow."

"Neither will Lord Sterling," Prince Kenneth said.

Aileen stood up, "I will collect her and get her ready for the trip."

Before Prince Kenneth could say anything more, Aileen was out of the room and gone. He shook his head, but did not immediately return to working on the papers. He had a daughter and he had to consider her future.

The first thought that entered his mind was he could convince his father to postpone the wedding. His father would pay for the detective to come back to the village and restart his search for the hummingbird. King Drax would only try to get Prince Kenneth to marry Princess Priscilla if the mother of Isadora could not be found within a reasonable time period.

Prince Kenneth was happy he had a child and the wedding would be canceled, but he wished his hummingbird had not flown.

Rana closed the book and put it away. The other couple had already gone up to their room and everyone else was likely to be impatient to do the same as it was getting late into the night. Rana got to her feet. By the time she had reached the stairs, the young man Carter had talked to appeared with a lamp.

"This way to your room," he said. He led her up the stairs to the second door. He opened it before giving her the key. Her luggage was already inside, but her maid was not there. There was only one bed in the room, so Rana figured her maid must have been given a bed somewhere else.

"Good night," the young man said.

"Good night," Rana replied. He shut the door. She waited until she could hear his footsteps on the stairs before locking the door.

Rana went through her bags until she found her nightgown. She changed into it and then climbed into bed. With her head against the soft pillow and her eyes threatening to close, Rana realized she had not seen Eustace since the incident with the woman in the marketplace. He must have fallen into a deep sleep if he had not been begging for any of her supper.

Oh well, Rana thought, he would be all right. She let her eyes close.

She was half asleep when she heard a thumping. It sounded like something large hitting the wall above her head. Moaning came through the wall to go along with the thumping. Ran folded the pillow over her ears as the screaming started. The pillow muffled the sounds a little, but not enough.

Finally, the noise stopped and Rana was able to lower the pillow back onto the bed. She relaxed and let herself start to drift off. She was just about asleep when the moaning started all over again. Rana pulled the pillow back over her ears and let the sounds become part of her dreams.

Rana woke up feeling like she had not slept. The curtains had been closed so she could not tell what time it was. It was the pounding on the door, which kept her from going back to sleep.

"Lady Rana?" her maid's voice called, "Lady Rana. We need to get going. Lady Rana?"

Rana sighed as she sat up. She really did not want to get up, but apparently she did not have the option of continuing to sleep. Rana climbed out of bed and let her maid into the room. Her maid immediately went to Rana's luggage and took out everything Rana would need to get dressed. Rana dressed while her maid packed everything away properly.

When Rana was ready, she and her maid took her luggage downstairs. Rana was given a basket with breakfast in it when she paid for her stay. Then everything was loaded back into the carriage, along with Rana and her maid. Carter got up in the driver's seat and the carriage started to move. Rana watched out the window for several minutes. She thought about trying to go to sleep, but she had never been very successful at sleeping in a moving carriage. So, Rana took out The Prince and the Rogue again.

The next day about mid-morning, Prince Kenneth sat out to a bench in the front garden. He was enjoying the garden and relaxing rather than focusing on the paperwork he had brought with him. The fall colours shone in the bright sunshine. The flowers were still blooming, but the bushes and trees had started turning red. Another few weeks and the garden would be put to bed for the winter. Prince Kenneth had not enjoyed being out in the fall in several years because they always reminded him of the night in the orchard after he and the hummingbird had slipped out of the ball.

Aileen came through the gate with the girl in tow and a bag in her hand. She had started toward the house before seeing Prince Kenneth on the bench. Aileen changed her course and headed straight towards him. The girl looked scared and dragged her feet. Aileen stopped a few feet from the bench.

"This is Isadora," Aileen said pushing the girl forward before placing the bag beside her. Isadora stayed there and just looked up at Prince Kenneth.

"She will be much better off with you," Aileen said before turning and walking away. Prince Kenneth did not bother to watch her go, or attempt to call her back. He turned his attention to Isadora and smiled at her.

"I am your father," Prince Kenneth said holding out his hand. Isadora hesitated for a moment before taking it. He led her over to sit on the bench beside him.

"What did Aileen tell you?" Prince Kenneth asked.

"She said I was not going to live with her anymore," Prince Kenneth could barely hear the girl, "She said I was going away, but she did not say much else."

"She was right," Prince Kenneth said, "You are going to come home to live with me as my daughter. I live in the palace in the capital city, which is a three day ride from here. You will get to ride in a wagon as we will be traveling with a caravan. Your grandfather will be very surprised to meet you, but once he had accepted your existence he will welcome you. Do you have any questions?"

"What happened to my mother?" Isadora asked, "Aileen said she abandoned me."

"I do not know," Prince Kenneth said, "I have searched for her for a long time now. I doubt she felt she had any choice about leaving you. She is not the type of person who would leave something as precious as you without a good reason. Okay?"

"Okay," Isadora nodded.

"Any other questions?" Prince Kenneth asked.

"Do you want me?" Isadora asked.

"Of course, I want you," Prince Kenneth answered, "I only learned of you yesterday or you would already live at the palace."

"Do I get my own room, or do I have to share with someone?" Isadora asked, "Because Aileen's house is not very big and I have had to share the bedroom with her. She snores and it makes it hard to sleep."

"The palace is big enough for you to have your own room," Prince Kenneth answered.

"Good," Isadora said. Prince Kenneth smiled, but did not say anymore because there were more people at the gate. There were four wagons and half a dozen riders. They pulled up to the entrance of the house and parked.

The butler came out and talked to the leader, who had gotten down from his horse to go up the steps. The leader was a large man with flowing robes and a turban. Prince Kenneth recognized the clothes as those from the neighbouring land behind the range of mountains to the east. Though he had never been there, Prince Kenneth had heard about the desert conditions and the clothing the citizens wore there. Much of the rest of group wore similar outfits. There were a few in trousers and shirts. And three in black outfits. The three were on the same wagon. They had trousers which were tight at the ankle and top, but loose in between. Their shirts were also loose and they had hoods which covered their faces. One had a cloth which covered his mouth as well.

The butler and the leader talked for a few minutes while the rest of the group waited. The member of the group with the cloth over the person's mouth drew Prince Kenneth attention. The person sat in the driver's seat of the wagon. Despite studying the person for several minutes, Prince Kenneth could not tell whether the person was male or female. The other two in black were male and it was easy to see that. The leader went back to his horse and mounted. Two of the others on horses gathered close to him to receive their orders. Once he was finished talking to them, the leader went to the driver of each wagon to repeat the same orders.

The horse riders and wagons went the rest of the circle to arrive back at the gate. They left the property, but headed along the road back the way they had come. Likely they had a place they could set up camp for the night and come back tomorrow morning. The driver in black looked at Prince Kenneth and Isadora as they went passed. Prince Kenneth could not see the eyes of the person due to their hood. Then the caravan was gone.

"Are we going with them?" Isadora asked.

"Yes," Prince Kenneth answered.

"I always wanted to travel them," Isadora said, "They look like they go interesting places. Aileen never went anywhere, except from her home to the village and back. I was not even allowed to go along

the path in the forest.”

“I understand wanting to go on adventures,” Prince Kenneth said, “When I was your age I wanted to be a knight and go save people from dragons and evil wizards.”

“Did you ever do that?” Isadora asked.

“No,” Prince Kenneth answered, “It was explained to me about how dragons were not all bad and evil wizards were rare. The training to be a knight is also a lot more difficult than just putting on a suit of armour and going out on adventures. There is a much more expected of them, like purity and self-sacrifice. I could not be the moral compass needed for the role of being a knight.”

“Could I try being a knight?” Isadora asked.

“You could try,” Prince Kenneth answered, “But it is hard.”

“You tell me what to do and I will try it,” Isadora said.

“Okay,” Prince Kenneth said, “I will take on the role as your squire since the squire is the person who takes care of the knight. We need to find you some armour.”

“Where are we going to find some armour?” Isadora asked.

“Maybe Lord Sterling has some we can borrow,” Prince Kenneth answered standing up. Isadora stood up as well. Prince Kenneth picked up the bag. It was fairly light. He suspected there was not much more than a change of clothes in there.

Rana found herself staring out the window and the book fallen to her lap. The scenery outside did not register in her brain. The tiredness of too little sleep was starting to get to Rana. She would curl up on the seat, but she knew sleeping in the carriage would leave her sick and feeling worse. Rana was better off losing herself in the book. She opened it up and started reading again.

Prince Kenneth woke up, but was not quite sure what disturbed him. He could hear the two on watch talking quietly, but it was not loud enough to interrupt sleep. Prince Kenneth lay still and concentrated on the other noises. There was nothing. He sat up and looked around. The camp fire was still burning, casting enough light to see within the circle of wagons. Anything outside the circle of light was dark.

The men on watch were silent. Prince Kenneth also noticed the thieves were awake. He pulled out his sword and got ready for whatever was out there. Alim sat up and looked to do the same. Slowly the rest were woken, either by the sounds of everyone else or by someone waking them.

Prince Kenneth saw the female thief gently wake Isadora and keep her quiet. They crawled under a wagon where they were hidden from sight and hopefully out of danger.

Everyone else got to their feet and ready to fight. Nothing appeared to be out there, but there was a sense of danger approaching. Prince Kenneth took a deep breath in readiness and found a foul odor. He sniffed again. It smelled like unwashed beings and a garbage pile.

"Goblins," Prince Kenneth muttered as he took a firmer grip on his sword. Alim heard him and also smelled the air. He nodded in agreement. Goblins were silent in their footfalls, but the vibrations still went through the ground which was likely what had disturbed the group. It must have been a large group of goblins out there.

The members of the caravan formed a circle facing outward from the fire. They searched for any sign of the enemy, but the darkness did not provide anything. The smell however did get stronger.

Suddenly there were goblins coming at the group from every direction. Prince Kenneth was able to block the first attack and strike the goblin down. The next one took a little longer to dispatch, but Prince Kenneth was able to do it while avoiding attacks from other goblins near him.

Goblins were short creatures with brown skin stretched thinly in some places and sagging in others. They wore either crudely stitched leather clothes or whatever they could scavenge. Their weapons were rusty and sometimes poisoned. The goblins had no valuables, or *anything else. Well, the goblins do not keep any items on them, but they must hide them somewhere because when they defeat someone everything is stripped away even the body.*

Prince Kenneth worked hard to keep an open space, but there was too many goblins converging on him. They definitely were not taking turns, instead they seemed to be swinging all at once. Prince Kenneth fought hard and was managing to avoid being hit. One of Alim's men across the fire from Prince Kenneth had fallen down. As soon as the man had collapsed the goblins switched their attention to the remaining opponents, rather than finishing him off.

The grass was getting slippery from goblin blood leaking from the bodies piling up as more and more goblins arrived to challenge the campers. The goblins continued their charge over the bodies of their comrades and the group from the caravan had no choice but to try and keep their balance.

One of Prince Kenneth's guards dropped from a blow of a goblin blade. As soon as he was lying on the ground the goblins ignored him and spread out to attack the rest of the group. Prince Kenneth found he had to be careful of goblins coming at him from all sides now as a few came through the holes around the fire. Another one of Alim's men was not paying enough attention and was struck by a goblin's weapon, which created another gap around the fire.

Prince Kenneth tried to keep his feet in places where there was less blood. He worked hard to keep all goblins weapons far enough away he was not likely to be injured. From the corner of his eye, Prince Kenneth saw Lord Sterling being overwhelmed by the goblins and go down. Those goblins immediately left the body alone and moved on to attacking the rest of them.

Alim fell to his knees due to a goblin blade connecting with his head, but he managed to keep swinging. He disappeared from Prince Kenneth's sight because of the crowd of goblins around him, but Prince Kenneth knew he was still active because the goblins did not disperse.

Prince Kenneth kept track of the horde of goblins around Alim, but he never saw the point where Alim went down. Something slammed into the back of his head. The goblins stopped attacking as he stood stunned for a moment. His sword slipped from his fingers and dropped onto the grass. He fell to his knees and then forward to lie beside his sword. Prince Kenneth saw the goblins go off to attack the others still standing. He wanted to check on whether Isadora was okay, but his brain said enough and he blacked out.

The carriage stopped and the sun was still high in the sky. Rana looked out the window and saw they had arrived at the estate. The estate had a main building with two extensions on each side. The whole building was made of worked stone. The front had ivy growing on the front so it was hard to tell the condition of the place. The garden looked slightly taken care of but needed a proper pruning. Leaves from the fall still littered the steps. The windows were shuttered, except for one in the right wing on the second floor. Parts of the roof looked ready to cave in.

Carter had gotten down as well as the guards. As Carter was opening the door of the carriage, a man came out of the front door. He was grey haired and had a limp. His brown clothes were patched in more places than not. The man arrived at the bottom step as Rana stepped down from the carriage.

"Duchess Rana," the man bowed, "Word of your arrival came yesterday. Rooms are being made up now."

"Good," Rana said, "It does not look like this place has been kept up."

"Very little funds have been left to keep it up with," the man replied, "And when the former owner died we only stayed because we had no other place to go. When the king took over, we were provided with enough to continue to do basic upkeep."

"That will change as of now," Rana said, "I will be staying here for a while and will be providing the money to fix this place up to be a comfortable residence."

"Yes, Duchess Rana," the man bowed again.

"Lady Rana," Rana said, "How many people are living here currently?"

"Just my wife, my daughter, my daughter's husband, and myself," the man answered.

"And your name is?" Rana asked.

"Selwyn," the man replied.

"Well, Selwyn," Rana said, "Give my maid and Carter directions to my room, so they can take my bags up. Then you can give me a tour so I can see what all needs to be done."

"Yes, Lady Rana," Selwyn bowed again before turning to Carter, who had started taking down the trunks with the help of Duard. Havard stood by waiting. Rana's maid had gathered the bags from inside the carriage and was waiting for instructions.

Selwyn gave directions before leading the way into the house. Rana and Havard followed him inside. The main part of the house was the sitting room, dining room, kitchen, and large entrance. The left wing had the ballroom, library, office, and solar. The right wing was single bedrooms and suites for those living there as well as guests. The servants' rooms were on the first floor and the other rooms were on the floors above.

Rana could see plenty of work that needed to be done, but it was getting close to supper time and Selwyn had other jobs to do. So, Rana stayed in her room as she waited for the call to eat. Her maid was busy doing her best to unpack and make the room livable, but the room like the rest of the house needed work. Duard and

Havard had their own rooms a little farther down the hallway while Rana's maid was in the room next to hers. Selwyn and his family lived in the servants' rooms, which were right below Rana's room.

Rana found the chair beside the window to be comfortable and the sun shone in the window to light up the pages of the book she had taken out. She was not needed for anything and she would be called when supper was ready. Rana opened it up to the place where she had left off.

Isadora had watched her father fall to the ground, but the thief, Mar, had held her back from running to him. Mar had kept a firm grip on Isadora throughout the whole fight. The goblins had not stripped any of the wagons even after they dragged the bodies off. None of the goblins even sniffed around them for anything of value.

Mar held Isadora still until they could no longer hear the goblins. Isadora went over to where her father had been. There were plenty of goblin bodies, but no trace of Prince Kenneth. She looked around the camp site. Aside from the wagons and remains of the fire, there was nothing remaining of the comfort that had been.

"Come," Mar said. Isadora turned to see the thief had gotten two cloaks from the wagon and was standing near the trail the goblins had left.

"But they're gone," Isadora said.

"They are all still alive," Mar said, "And without our help they will not stay that way. Come on and help me."

Isadora glanced back at the camp. Without her father there was nothing left there she valued. She turned back walked to Mar, who put the smaller cloak around her shoulders. Mar put her own cloak on before taking Isadora's hand. They followed the trail the goblins left along with the smell.

Just before dawn Mar and Isadora found themselves within sight of a black tower deep in a forested area. The trees stood at a distance of the base of the tower as if they were afraid to grow too close. Mar had let Isadora rest and have something to eat while she checked out the tower. Isadora sat on a rock and watched the tower. There was no visible activity around it, but even she could tell by the smell that this was where the goblins had taken her father and the other men.

Mar slipped back to being next to Isadora, but waited for Isadora to finish eating before she spoke. Isadora ate slowly because she believed it filled her stomach more than if she ate fast. And the widow barely had enough to feed both of them most days, so anything to make a meal more filling was desirable.

"Ready?" Mar asked once Isadora finished chewing. Isadora nodded.

"Stay close to me," Mar said, "If we get separated stay quiet and hide best you can. I will come find you on the way out. I know you have been practicing using a sword, but it is best if you do not engage the goblins in combat. They call more to their aid and can quickly overwhelm you."

Isadora nodded. She was ready. Mar held out her gloved hand and Isadora took the hand as she got up. They moved swiftly, being careful to stay in the shadows, along the path to the door of the tower. There was a large, two storey, steel door, but Mar went around to a side door, which was much smaller and made of wood. Mar let go of Isadora's hand and pushed the door open a small amount. The stench of goblins assaulted them, but there was no sound of goblins being near the door.

Mar poked her in head inside to look around. Her body followed shortly and then she signaled Isadora to follow her. Inside was dark, musty, and rank. It had stone walls and floor which held moisture which came from piles lying on the floor. Isadora could not identify them and Mar rushed her so she had no chance to get close enough to try. The room they had entered was about eight feet across and round with a doorway on the other side.

Isadora followed Mar through the doorway and into a much

bigger room. This room was the place the steel door led to as it was in the wall to their right. This room was most of the width of the tower with another doorway across from this one and a fourth door across from the steel one. The room was had piles all over the room. They looked like cloth, but there was other things mixed in. Again Mar kept Isadora from investigating them. There was no furniture, but a couple piles looked like they might contain wood. There were no goblins in sight, but the smell was strong. All the light in the room came from two lanterns hung high up on the walls. There may have been more up there, but only two were lit.

Mar picked her way through the room toward the fourth door. Isadora followed close behind her. Mar made no sound as she moved while Isadora could not help that her borrowed armour creaked and her shoes made a shuffling noise. The large room was dead silent; no wind whistling through it, no animals scampering about, or thumps of goblins. It gave Isadora a chill and she worked hard to be quieter, but she was not very successful. Mar never looked back, or seemed worried about the amount of noise she was making.

They reached the door and Mar pushed it open. The smell of goblins got stronger and there was more light coming through. Mar checked it for goblins before going through and letting Isadora inside. Mar closed the door behind them. This area was a landing with a barred, steel door straight across from them and stairs on either side. The right set was going up and the left set was going down. There was the sound of goblins coming from the right and there was no sounds coming from the left.

Mar put her hands to her head and moaned softly before falling to her knees. Isadora stepped closer to her, but was not sure what to do. The only person she had seen do such things was the blacksmith's daughter and no one paid her any attention when she did. Isadora also did not want to ask Mar if she was all right for fear that the goblins would hear them and investigate the sound. She placed her hand on Mar's shoulder. Mar shook her head as if she was trying to get rid of something. Then she looked at Isadora and patted her hand.

"It is okay," Mar whispered as she got to her feet. She seemed to be back to normal. It has always taken the blacksmith's daughter several minutes before she could do anything.

"I need you to go down the stairs," Mar pointed to the left, "And free the men."

"But how?" Isadora started.

"Use this key," Mar handed Isadora a key, "There should be no any goblins down there to deal with. I will meet up with you."

"Okay," Isadora took the key, but she was not sure about leaving Mar, especially after what just happened.

"Go," Mar said pushing Isadora toward the stairs going down. Isadora continued forward and started down the stairs. Unlike the rest of the floor, the stairs were clear of the piles. No sounds came up the stairs from anything that might be below and the smell of goblins was still strong. Isadora looked back at Mar, who was still standing there. She was watching Isadora go, not recovering from whatever happened. Isadora nodded and turned back around. She could do this. She could help her father, if he was down here.

Rana looked up from her book to where her maid was standing in the doorway.

"Yes?" Rana asked.

"Supper is ready," her maid said.

"Okay," Rana said standing up. She left the book on the chair and followed her maid out of the room.

Selwyn seemed a little nervous as everyone was seated at the big table instead of Rana sitting alone in the dining room while the rest were in the kitchen. However, his wife seemed completely unaware that this was not an appropriate arrangement. Rana sat down in the place, which appeared to be for her and said nothing about eating alone. Once everyone else was seated, they started to eat.

After supper, everyone headed off to their own activities. Selwyn went off before Rana could stop him and ask whether they could discuss the plans for the repairs. However, since he was busy at the moment, Rana decided they could discuss the repairs in the morning. Instead, she went back up to her room and sat down on the chair again. Rana picked up the book again and opened it to the where she left off.

The smell was the first thing that hit Prince Kenneth as he regained consciousness. It was like there was a goblin sitting right next to him. But when Prince Kenneth opened his eyes he found no goblins in sight. Instead there were bars along the middle of the floor in this room, which might have been large if all of it could be seen. The only light source was two torches on either side of the doorway, which barely made it passed the bars and definitely did not get to the far corners.

It looked like the goblins did not venture into the far corners either as Prince Kenneth and the rest of the men from the caravan had all been dumped within a foot of the bars. They were all lying or sitting in the light. All of them were present. The only ones missing were the thief and Isadora. Prince Kenneth hoped that the thief had enough sense to take Isadora to the capital and get his father to send reinforcements to help them. It meant he and the rest would sit here for a while, but it also meant that his daughter would be safe.

Prince Kenneth sat up. None of those who are already conscious said anything. Everyone was banged up from the fight and looked in need of medical attention, but without a doctor or supplies they would not receive it. Alim was lying close to Prince Kenneth and looked worst of all for injuries. His olive skin was pale against the dark red of the dried blood which had seeped from the wounds on his face. His clothes were tattered and there was a large bruise on the side of his head. Prince Kenneth reached over and checked to make sure Alim had a pulse. He was relieved to find one and that it felt normal.

There was shuffling sound. Prince Kenneth looked at the men, but all were still. The sound was coming from the darkness farther back. He wondered what else was locked up with them as he searched the dark for whatever was moving. A moment passed before a man came out into the light. He might have been tall once, but now was hunched over. He dragged his left foot behind him as if it did not work anymore. His cloak was grey with many holes in it, it showed the remains of his once white shirt and black trousers. His hair and beard were overgrown and matted with dirt. He blinked at the brightness of the light as he looked over the group.

"Drax?" his voice was rough with disuse, but there was still some sense of strength he no longer had.

"I am Prince Kenneth," Prince Kenneth answered, "King Drax is my father."

"I am honoured," the man's bow was awkward, "Though I wish your visit was under better circumstances on both sides."

"And you are?" Prince Kenneth asked.

"I am Lord Freund," the man answered, "And this is the tower given to my family by your great-grandfather."

"How long have you suffered here with the goblins living here?" Prince Kenneth asked.

"Years," Lord Freund answered, "How many, I do not know."

"Come sit," Prince Kenneth gestured to space beside Alim, "Tell me how this happened." Lord Freund shuffled his way to the place indicated and lowered himself to the stone floor.

"My household and I had just gotten back from the masquerade at the capital when there was a visitor," Lord Freund's voice got a little stronger as he spoke, "The man did not identify himself, nor did he take down the hood of his cloak. He told me that I should turn against the throne and ally myself with him. I refused and had him tossed out, but not before he warned that such

action would cause a curse to come upon this tower. I did not believe him until the shade moved into the room at the top of the tower. Shortly after the shade moved in, all my people began to get sick. The main room of the tower became a hospital and those who were not sick at the beginning tended to those who were. I thought about sending a message to the capital, but by the time anyone came near enough for me to pass on the message everyone, except me, was sick.

"When people started dying, I decided that I had to get a message to King Drax. I opened the door to the tower and found it surrounded by camps of goblins. There was no way out if I wanted to survive. After that I just took care of my people as I watched them die and waited to get sick. I was not as lucky as my people in that I did not get sick.

"When the last of my people died, the doors opened and the goblins poured in. The shade welcomed them. I fought for as long as I could and as hard as I could. That is how I injured my leg. When I could not fight anymore, the shade had the goblins throw me down here, put the bars in, and leave me here. I do not know what has happened since then, but the goblins and likely the shade are still here. They brought all of you in a few hours ago."

"I remember you being at the masquerade ball about six years ago," Prince Kenneth said, "But I do not remember you being there since."

"Six years," Lord Freund said, "It seems much longer."

Alim opened the eye that was not swollen shut and looked around without moving. Once he understood where they were, he slowly sat up. He did not look well, but he did not lie back down.

"We need to figure out how to get out of here," Prince Kenneth said.

"All our weapons are gone," Lord Jegger said, "Along with all our other equipment."

"We have two missing from our number," Alim said.

"We do," Prince Kenneth replied, "And I hope they have enough sense to go for help."

"*You do not know Mar then,*" one of the male thieves said, "*She does not have enough sense to get out of a sand storm.*"

"*She not only survived the sand storm,*" Alim said, "*She rescued that Lord and Lady who had gotten lost. They paid us all handsomely for the help getting back to civilization.*"

"*Can one of you two open the lock?*" Prince Kenneth asked the two thieves.

"*Can't,*" the second thief answered, "*All our equipment is in the wagon. The lock needs a key and there is nothing around here looks like it could be useful.*"

"*This cellar used to be for storage,*" Lord Freund said, "*But it was emptied as part of an inventory and clean out we were doing before everyone got sick.*"

Creak of amour came from the doorway causing everyone to look over. The figure was not quite into the light from the torches, but it was too small to be a goblin unless it was a weak one given the job of bringing food. The problem with that was the figure did not carry anything big enough to be food. The footfalls were quiet and the figure was trying to be quiet despite the creaking of the armour.

Finally the figure got close enough to the light they could see that is was Isadora. She was hesitant as she came down the stairs and into the cellar. Joy and fear went through Prince Kenneth's heart. The thief, Mar, apparently did not have enough common sense to get the girl to safety, or even keep Isadora close to her.

Isadora looked around the cellar and having assuring herself that there were no goblins about, then ran to the gate in the bars. Prince Kenneth got to his feet and went over to the gate.

"*Where is Mar?*" Prince Kenneth asked as Isadora took out a key.

"*She is up the stairs,*" Isadora answered, "*She needs help. She was holding her head and told me to go and let you out.*" Isadora put the key into the lock and turned it. There was a clicking sound and the door opened with a squeak. Everyone else climbed to their feet, except Alim who did not try to move.

"Is there an armory?" Prince Kenneth asked Lord Freund.

"On the upper floor," Lord Freund answered.

"That is where the goblins are," Isadora said.

"We will have to be careful," Lord Jegger said, "Collect any weapons we can as we go."

Everyone started toward the stairs, except Prince Kenneth and Isadora. She looked at him.

"I need you to stay here and protect Alim," Prince Kenneth said, "He should not move."

"I will," Isadora said.

"Thank you," Prince Kenneth said. Isadora took the key out of the lock and put it in her pocket before sitting down near Alim. Prince Kenneth followed the men up the stairs.

The stairwell twisted up with no torches or lanterns to light the way. They went around a pole to the left. The stairs were wide enough for two people to walk side by side, but Prince Kenneth kept his hand on the left wall so as not to trip. The light from the torches at the bottom faded away and none came from above making it dark as a moonless night. Prince Kenneth could hear the men ahead of him making their way through the darkness with shuffling steps. When the footfalls became more confident, Prince Kenneth knew there must be some light coming from the top of the stairs.

Another loop around the pole and Prince Kenneth found the light filtering down from the torches. A little bit more and they were all standing in an alcove with another set of stairs ahead of them with a steel door to their right which stood open. On the floor were piles of fabric, metal, and bones. Prince Kenneth bent down and examined the one at the top of the stairs. He quickly realized that it was what was left of Lord Freund's people.

Lord Freund stopped Lord Jegger from picking up a sword that was near the top of one of the piles.

"Take it only if you wish to be cursed," Lord Freund said, "The armory is farther up." Lord Freund pointed up to the stairs going up. Lord Jegger looked briefly at the sword again as if

wondering to himself whether it was worth it to pick the sword up, but must have decided that is was not because he left the sword where it was.

Prince Kenneth glanced into the main room of the tower to see more piles that had been people. It made goose bumps rise on his skin. His father knew there were enemies, but the level of power was much more than his father acknowledged. And if this all happened six year ago, they likely have gained even greater power. Prince Kenneth knew they had to clear out the tower quickly and get back to the capital.

Lord Jegger and the rest of the men from the capital headed up the stairs with the men from the caravan following them. Lord Freund, Lord Sterling, and the two thieves stayed with Prince Kenneth.

"We have no weapons and there is a shade up there," Lord Sterling said, "Do we have any way of fighting a shade?"

"We need to get up there and find that other thief," Prince Kenneth said, "And if possible clear the tower. Lord Freund will have to come to the capital because his people are dead, but I do not want to leave this place full of goblins for any unsuspecting innocence to encounter. The shade is dangerous and leaves this tower an enemy foothold in our kingdom."

"But what can we do without weapons?" Lord Sterling asked, "And how do we deal with the shade?"

"We will figure it out," Prince Kenneth said, "Now we might as well follow them up, before they run into a bad situation."

Everyone looked up the stairs at the group which was disappearing out of sight. The group disappeared into the darkness. Prince Kenneth took a deep breath and started up. The second group followed him up.

The sun had gone down too far for Rana to read any further, so she closed the book. Her maid had been waiting with Rana's nightgown ready and as soon as Rana moved from the chair her maid closed the curtains. Rana changed and got ready for bed.

"Let Selwyn know that I would like to meet with him after breakfast to discuss the repairs," Rana told her maid.

"Yes, Lady Rana," her maid said before leaving the room and closing the door behind her. Rana lay down on the bed and got ready to sleep. It had been a long day of traveling, which was always tiresome. Rana was sure there was nothing to disturb her sleep here. After a quick run through of what she was going to have to do the next day, Rana closed her eyes and relaxed into her pillow.

The creaking started out softly. So softly Rana almost did not notice it. But then it got louder and faster. Rana wondered for a moment where it was coming from before she realized it was coming from the room below hers. Rana once again folded the pillow over her ears and hoped it would block the sound.

RANA HELPS PLAN THE REPAIRS, WHICH START OUT GREAT

After breakfast, Rana had Selwyn join her in the study, which despite appearing to have a leak in the ceiling, seemed stable. Selwyn sat down in the chair opposite the one Rana sat down in, so they were across the desk from each other.

"What exactly did you want to discuss, Lady Rana?" Selwyn asked once they were settled.

"I know you were just going to hire a few men and merely patch things up," Rana said, "But I think this place needs more work than that. I am going to live here for a while and would rather make it livable than just good enough for a summer home. Also, there needs to be some improvements to the place."

"Very well," Selwyn said, "What exactly did you have in mind?"

Rana went to outline what she was thinking as she did

so she wrote it out on a piece of paper. After listening to her and seeing what she had written out, Selwyn made some suggestions based on what he knew about the building and the land around it. By the time lunch was ready, they had come up with a good plan for renovations to the house and Selwyn was much more comfortable with Rana. Selwyn was going to head out after lunch to gather supplies as well as men to do the work.

Lunch was quiet as everyone was still getting used to each other. Rana did not mind. She did talk about her plans to the group so everyone would know what was going on. Everyone expressed contentment at the plans, even though they understood the next while would be a time of discomfort. The plans did involve starting with the left wing and working to the right wing, but it did not mean people would have the change how they did things depending on where the work was being done.

After lunch, Rana found a chair outside under the shade of one of the trees and sat there with her book to enjoy the afternoon as she had nothing else to do with her time. Except maybe write a letter to her brother, which she was putting off. So, she opened the book and started reading.

Prince Kenneth managed to keep the goblin attacking him at bay with his fists until he could disarm it and grab the rusty blade it had been using. The men around him were doing similar, although most of the group who followed Lord Jegger had gotten weapons by now. The one guard had not managed to get a weapon at all before one of the goblins had gotten to him. Lord Freund was having trouble getting passed the doorway, but he was keeping any goblins from leaving.

They had gone up the stairs and found where the goblins had been living. There had to be another area, higher in the tower.

Prince Kenneth thought it might be through the door on the other side of the room, but he had not been able to get through the goblins to get to the door. But now that he had a sword it should be easier.

A rather feminine scream cut through the air, but the goblins did not pause. Prince Kenneth fought harder to get through to the door. None of the company had come upon the thief, so she must have been on the higher floor. Prince Kenneth was not sure how she got passed the goblins, but she was a thief. The scream was cut off suddenly and a laughter filled the air. It was a warped, directionless laughter which vibrated through the whole tower. Prince Kenneth felt the chill through his whole body.

There was a cry from behind him. Lord Freund had fallen to his knees and was clutching his chest. Prince Kenneth was torn between continuing towards the door and going back to help Lord Freund. Lord Sterling ran through the goblin he was fighting and made his way toward Lord Freund. Seeing that help was on its way, Prince Kenneth continued moving toward the door, though he was checking back to see what was happening.

Lord Sterling reached Lord Freund and helped him to his feet. Lord Freund leaned against the wall for a moment, but seemed to be all right. Finally he was able to stand on his own feet and help out from his place in the doorway.

Prince Kenneth was getting closer to the door on the far side of the room when the laughter stopped. If it was not for the ringing of metal weapons against each other, the silence would have left him wondering whether he could hear at all. Even the noise of battle was dim and far away. Prince Kenneth found he could hear his own thoughts again, but they were scrambled and it took a moment to let them settle. The only thing that saved him was the goblins were having the same trouble.

Once his head was clear enough, Prince Kenneth went back to taking out goblins. The goblins had been putting up a good fight, but their numbers were down from the fight at the caravan camp and they did not have the same type of help. Prince Kenneth had managed to get more than half way across the room with the rest of the men close behind him. Lord Freund was still on the landing outside the door, but he was fighting any goblins that strayed out too close to him.

The walls of the tower began to shake causing panic among the goblins and some of the men. Using the distraction, Prince Kenneth made the last push to the door. The goblins were off guard enough that he reached his goal. The door was not locked, but it was heavy and Prince Kenneth had to wait until Lord Jegger reached him to help open it. They pushed the door open.

Instead of stairs, the door led into a small alcove. There was a single fire burning in a metal container set in the middle of the space with white paint circles and lines on the floor around. Mar was on her knees in the first circle holding her left arm to her chest and mumbling. The shade was silently screaming as it was clawing at the walls and floor trying to stay out of the fist-sized amethyst which was sucking him in.

Prince Kenneth and Lord Jegger started to enter the room.

"Stop," Mar said holding her hand. Prince Kenneth stopped, but Lord Jegger took a step further inside before stopping. His foot was barely outside the white paint. Once they had both stopped, Mar dropped her hand to her side and started mumbling again. Lord Jegger was starting to forward again, but Prince Kenneth grabbed his arm and pulled him back.

The shade was struggling to stay free. It reached a point where the shade was managing to avoid being sucked in farther. Mar put both hands on the floor and speaking louder. The shaking of the tower got worse, but the shade was once again being sucked into the gemstone.

Prince Kenneth noticed two holes in Mar's sleeve, one on each side of the sleeve. The skin, he could see through the cloth, was red, swollen, and looked like it had been burned. Prince Kenneth looked up at the shade, which was silently screaming as it was sucked into the gemstone. The shade tried to grab on to the stone floor with its extra long fingers, but it could not get a grip. The head disappeared into the gemstone followed by the arms. Its fingers were still trying to hold on to something as they were pulled in last.

The tower stopped shaking. Noise of the fight with the goblins turned into the goblins fleeing. Mar half collapsed to the floor where she sat trying to get her breathe back.

Lord Jegger stepped toward the gemstone.

"Do not touch it," Mar shouted as he leaned down toward it. Lord Jegger backed off as he looked at her.

"If you touch it the shade will be let out again," Mar said. Lord Jegger backed away to stand near Prince Kenneth again.

Mar slowly got her breath back before she moved closer to the gemstone. She placed her hands on either side of it and started whispering in a language no one else understood.

There was the sound of footsteps and Alim limped into the room with Isadora right behind him. He stopped at the sight of Mar. She finished whispering and picked up the gemstone, which she slipped into her pocket before turning to the men standing in the doorway.

"Always nice to have a shade for a pet," Mar said. Not being able to see her face, Prince Kenneth could not tell if she was trying to be funny. There was more tiredness than amusement in her tone.

Mar's legs did not want to hold her up but she quickly straightened up. Alim stepped into the room and offered his hand. She took a step toward him. Her knees were close to buckling, but Mar managed to reach him. Alim supported her the rest of the way out of the room.

"Come now, we need to get back to the wagons," Alim said as he and Mar supported each other as they headed for the stairs. Prince Kenneth and Lord Jegger looked at each other in confusion. Isadora followed behind Alim and the thief.

When they reached the top of the stairs. Lord Fruend offered his arm to support Mar. She accepted and the three went down the stairs together with Isadora following behind.

Prince Kenneth shrugged and headed down after them. Lord

Jegger and the rest of the men followed him. The three led the way down the stairs, through the main hall, and through the large steel door. Once everyone was through, Lord Fruend shut and locked the doors. Only once he was finished did they start again.

Voices caused Rana to look up from the book. Selwyn's wife and daughter-in-law were talking as they worked in the garden. Rana watched them for several minutes. They seemed to enjoy working in their garden, which Rana understood because she has seen plenty of people who loved to work with plants. She had never been much in getting her hands dirty, but she had her own ways of relaxing. Rana went back to the adventures of the characters in her book.

King Drax was seated on his throne when the group entered the throne room. Also in attendance was the princess to whom Prince Kenneth was engaged. But Reginald was missing. Prince Kenneth was not sure whether that was a good thing or not because sometimes it meant Reginald was creating problems.

Prince Kenneth bowed to King Drax along with the rest of the group.

"Rise," King Drax said, "And give your report."

"I went to the village as requested," Prince Kenneth said, "Lord Sterling agreed to come back to court with me. We decided to ride back with Alim's caravan. Along the way we stopped for the night in a place we thought was safe and were attacked by goblins. They overpowered us and took us to Lord Fruend's tower, where we were locked in a cell in the cellar. We escaped and dealt with the goblins, as well as the shade who was controlling them. We brought back Lord Fruend back to tell his tale. The rest of the trip was uneventful." Prince Kenneth stepped back. King Drax had seen Isadora and his expression suggested he knew there was more to tell, but he let Prince Kenneth step aside.

"*Lord Fruend,*" *King Drax said.*

Lord Fruend stepped forward with a bow.

"*It is nice to see you back at court, my friend,*" *King Drax said, "Though the circumstance does not sound good. Please relate your tale.*"

"*Thank you, Your Majesty,*" *Lord Fruend said and then repeated the same story he had told Prince Kenneth and the rest back in the tower's cellar. King Drax listened and his expression grew more worried. Finally Lord Fruend finished his story and stepped back with a bow.*

"*Thank you, Lord Fruend,*" *King Drax said, "Your news is troubling, but it is very good to have you back at court. Rooms will be made up for you and we will send guards back to the tower to clean it out properly for your return. Though we wish for you to stay until some issues get resolved.*"

"*I will stay as long as you need, Your Majesty,*" *Lord Fruend replied and bowed.*

"*Thank you, Lord Fruend, you have our gratitude,*" *King Drax said before turning to Lord Sterling. Lord Sterling stepped forward and bowed.*

"*Thank you for coming as we requested,*" *King Drax said.*

"*Always your willing servant, Your Majesty,*" *Lord Sterling replied. He bowed again before stepping back.*

"*Now we have dealt with most of the business from this trip,*" *King Drax said, "We ask Prince Kenneth to introduce his guest.*"

"*Yes, Sire,*" *Prince Kenneth stepped forward while dragging Isadora with him. They both bowed.*

"*This is Isadora. She has been living in the village, but with your permission will move into the palace,*" *Prince Kenneth said.*

"*Why should we grant such a request?*" *King Drax asked.*

"*Because she is my daughter,*" *Prince Kenneth answered. The whole court went quiet. King Drax studied Isadora for a few minutes, which made her uncomfortable but she endured it. Princess Priscilla glared at the girl, but she could not actually do so because of the distance between them.*

"You understand that by taking her into the palace you are declaring that she is your heir," King Drax said, "And other agreements are no longer valid."

"I do," Prince Kenneth answered, "I accept responsibility in this matter."

"Very well," King Drax said, "We grant the permission for the child to move into the palace."

There was light applauding in the throne room, but most were still in shock over Prince Kenneth's announcement. Princess Priscilla looked angry enough to curse Prince Kenneth into an early grave, but she worked to hide it as quickly as she could.

"The steward will make up rooms near your own," King Drax said, "And the girl will be found servants and tutors as soon as possible. Princess Priscilla, we are sorry for wasting your time, but the engagement is annulled. We will find a way to send you home as soon as possible."

"Yes, Your Majesty," Princess Priscilla said. Her tone was not as calm as she was attempting to make it, but King Drax ignored it.

"Welcome Isadora," King Drax said.

"Thank you, Your Majesty," Isadora replied. She stepped back with Prince Kenneth.

"As you all appear to need time to get ready for supper, we dismiss the court," King Drax announced. Everyone bowed as King Drax rose and left the throne room. Then everyone else shuffled out. Prince Kenneth kept Isadora close to him and away from Princess Priscilla. However once outside the throne room the housekeeper took charge of Isadora leaving Prince Kenneth to deal other matters.

Rana found the afternoon has disappeared and the evening chill had arrived. She took her book with her when she went inside. She met with her maid coming out to call her for supper as she headed inside. Rana slipped the book into her pocket and followed her maid into the dining room.

Supper was another quiet affair. Rana was fine with that. It was nice to be where it was not as loud though she was sure she would miss the castle after a while. Right now she was satisfied with the quiet.

After supper, Rana went up to her room where she settled in the chair and lit the candle. She took the book out of her pocket and make sure she was comfortable before opening it up.

Prince Kenneth yawned as he slipped off his shirt. It had been a long journey and then a busy day. He had checked on Isadora, expecting her to be nervous about her first night in the palace, but she was already fast asleep. Prince Kenneth smiled to himself. He had already gotten one of the guards to protect her and continue her training to be a knight. As his heir, she would never get the chance to become a full knight, however if she knew how to fight then she could take any enemy by surprise. After all, who would think a six-year-old was handy with a sword.

The sky outside his window was purple and Prince Kenneth knew Manston, his valet, was going to bed in the next room. Nothing could keep Prince Kenneth awake much longer. He laid down on the bed and felt the luxury of being in his own bed with his own sheets as he stretched out. Closing his eyes, Prince Kenneth breathed in and slowly let it out as he drifted away.

A noise of a door opening and closing quietly caused Prince Kenneth open his eyes. There was the hummingbird and she was undressing as she walked toward the bed. She was naked by the time she slipped in beside him. The tiredness left Prince Kenneth as he reached for her. She welcomed him and moved closer. Neither talked as they touched. The warmth and smoothness of her skin beneath his lips made him feel like he had found the well from which he had been dying to drink.

"Prince Kenneth," there was someone banging on the door. Prince Kenneth opened his eyes and looked around. The hummingbird was gone and it looked like she had never been there, despite how real she felt just a moment ago. Manston called through the door again. Prince Kenneth shook his head to dislodge the dream before getting up. The sky outside was still dark with no sign of dawn.

Prince Kenneth opened the door to ask what was going on when he saw Manston's face was filled with panic and worry.

"King Drax has fallen ill," Manston said, "They are asking for you to come immediately."

"Of course," Prince Kenneth said. He had not taken off his trousers, so he just grabbed his shirt from where he had dropped it and slipped it over his head. Then he hurried from the room.

Prince Kenneth, Lord Jeggar, and Lord Sterling were sitting in chairs outside King Drax's bedroom. None of them were talking because none of them were sure exactly what to say. They had all visited King Drax and for a brief time had been able to talk to him, but King Drax had fallen asleep and no one wanted to disturb him.

A guard came down the hallway with Alim and the thief following him. Alim looked the same as Prince Kenneth has seen him earlier. At first Prince Kenneth thought the same as the thief, but then he noticed that she was not wearing any shoes. The guard brought Alim and the thief to where the men were standing before leaving again.

"What do you need?" Alim asked with a bow.

"My father could use your ability to heal," Prince Kenneth answered, "Anything you could do would be greatly appreciated."

"I will see what I can do," Alim said. He started toward the door when Prince Kenneth nodded. Alim opened the door and left it open while he went over to the bed. The thief stayed in the hallway with the men and watched from the doorway.

Alim knelt beside the bed before putting his hand on King Drax's forehead. He stayed in that position for several minutes. Finally he straightened up and removed his hand. After getting to his feet, Alim went back to the door.

"It appears that someone has used the jewel of Athum to poison him," Alim said, "There is nothing I can do. The only known cure is the leaves of the Kresk tree, which I do not have access to because to retrieve them is to court death."

"Where are the Kresk trees?" Prince Kenneth asked.

"In the land ruled by the dragon Shamus," Alim answered, "And only one has ever returned after venturing there."

"If they are still alive, their help would be needed," Lord Jeggar said, "Because otherwise whoever goes may not come back."

"I will go," Prince Kenneth said, "I am determined to find help for King Drax. Who is the person who survived venturing into the dragon Shamus's territory?"

"Mar," Alim pointed to the thief. If she thought anything about the situation, nothing in her posture suggested it and as usual he could not see her face. Her eyes were in shadow.

Lord Jeggar did not look happy at Alim's answer, however Prince Kenneth ignored him. If Mar was the only person who could lead him into the dangerous then he was not going to argue about her gender or her profession. Though he did wonder about why she had been there and how she managed to escape. He was likely to find some of that out as they traveled.

"Then we need to pack up and get moving," Prince Kenneth said, "The sooner we leave the sooner we can get back here."

"I will talk to the steward about what is required for the journey," Lord Jeggar said, "As well as get the guards ready. The guards and I will accompany you as far as the border to the territory."

"Very well," Prince Kenneth said before turning to the thief, "Will you be ready to go?"

"Of course, she will be," Alim said before the thief could say

anything, "She does not have any other work, so there is nothing to keep her from going."

Prince Kenneth was going to argue that the thief should answer, but the thief merely shrugged at Alim's words and gave no other acknowledgment to what was being asked of her.

"You need a horse," Lord Jeggar said.

"My wagon is ready to leave whenever you are," Mar replied. Lord Jeggar looked like he was going to say something against taking a wagon which would slow their travel.

"That will be fine," Prince Kenneth said. Lord Jeggar nodded to Prince Kenneth before heading off to talk to the steward. Alim gave Prince Kenneth a slight bow before he and the thief also left. Prince Kenneth stood there and looked in at his father, who was sleeping.

"Good luck," Lord Sterling said clapping Prince Kenneth on the back, "We will keep the kingdom running while you are gone as well as keep your father and Isadora safe."

"Thank you," Prince Kenneth said. He sighed before turning away and heading back to his room to repack his bag.

Rana was having trouble staying awake, so she put the book down. She got ready for the night and crawled into bed. She closed her eyes and let herself relax. As she started to drift into a pleasant dream, the creaking started. Rana sighed as she worked to ignore the noise and try to get back to the dream.

After breakfast the next morning, the workers showed up with the supplies. Rana talked with the foreman, who had already been briefed by Selwyn, as to what was happening. The foreman explained how much he expected to get done today and how long he believed the whole job would take. Rana was satisfied with his answers and found her chair under the tree where she could watch the workmen. Her maid joined her shortly after as there was little for her maid to do.

The workmen started taking down the walls of the left wing of the house. They left the support pieces but took out much of the rest of it. Selwyn and the rest of the servants had spent time yesterday and this morning cleaning up the rooms in the left wing. Most of the furniture and other stuff had been moved to some of the empty rooms in the right wing. Most of it would be moved back once the rooms were finished.

Rana enjoyed watching the workmen for a while and then decided she was bored. Taking out her book, Rana started to read.

Prince Kenneth, Lord Jeggar, the four guards, and Mar in her wagon had been traveling the night through and most of the morning. The thought among the group was that they could rest and get warm food at Lord Kenji's house. He was the first member of the council that the group would visit and they needed to find out why he had not responded to the king's summons to the capital. They also needed to know the fate of the messenger who had never returned. The residents of the last town before Lord Kenji's house told them that the messenger had passed safely through their village. He had stopped for something to eat, but then rushed off the see Lord Kenji. No one knew what had happened to him after that, for they had not seen him again and they had not seen Lord Kenji journey past.

Prince Kenneth had been watchful along the road coming up from the town, but had seen nothing to suggest the messenger had gotten into trouble. Everyone was on alert for fear of being attacked, but there did not seem to be anyone out there trying to attack them. Then the hedges, which were planted around Lord Kenji's property came into sight.

Prince Kenneth noticed Lord Jeggar and the guards relaxing at the sight of the familiar place. He, however, felt there was something wrong. Prince Kenneth could not tell if the thief felt anything because as usual her face was covered up with her clothing.

"Here we are at last," Lord Jeggar said as soon as the house became visible.

"It looks right," Prince Kenneth said, "But there is something wrong."

"Like Lord Kenji could be in trouble?" Lord Jeggar asked.

"No," Prince Kenneth answered, "But if I remember the place from the last time I was here, Lord Kenji's estate is another twenty minute ride from here."

Lord Jeggar stopped his horse to look over the house that looked exactly like Lord Kenji's house. Everyone else stopped at the same place to do the same.

"An illusion." Mar offers.

"A whole house?" one of the guards asked.

"Been done before," Mar answered, "Just need a powerful enough spell, or a powerful enough wizard."

"This might explain what happened to the messenger," Prince Kenneth said, "He tricked and went into this house thinking it was Lord Kenji's house. Then Lord Kenji not only does not get the message, he does not know anything of it."

"So, what do we do?" the guard asked.

"We can either go in and try and figure what is going on in there," Prince Kenneth said, "Or continue on to Lord Kenji's house for some rest and come back later to take down the illusion."

"I suggest we continue on to Lord Kenji's house," Lord Jeggar said, "Because if we want to figure out the illusion we need the rest and something to eat so that we can go in at our best rather than while we are tired and hungry."

"You are right," Prince Kenneth said, "Let us continue on."

The group started moving, but Prince Kenneth and Lord Jeggar watched the house for another minute before focusing on where they were headed.

Twenty minutes later another set of hedges came into sight. The company travels passed them and the house was soon visible again. This time there was movement from a gardener working in the gardens on the side of the cobblestones which made up the courtyard. The first house had not felt wrong, but this one definitely felt right.

Someone must have seen the group coming as not only did the steward come out to greet the group when they arrived at the steps, but so did Lord Kenji. He was a head shorter than everyone else, but his energy created the feeling that he was constantly bouncing. Lord Kenji kept his head shaved and preferred trousers with a shirt. Many times he would argue against the robes other members of the council thought they should wear because he felt it would make him look like a child's ball.

Prince Kenneth was the first to get down off his horse. Lord Kenji clasped Prince Kenneth in a hug. He did the same to Lord Jeggar when he had gotten off his horse.

"I am so glad to see you," Lord Kenji said, "It feels like so long since anyone has come out to see me. I was almost thinking I had been forgotten."

"How long has it been since someone has been out here?" Prince Kenneth asked.

"Four years at least," Lord Kenji answered after a moment of thought, "Why what is happening?" Lord Kenji became serious.

"We went passed a place that looked exactly like your house on the way here," Prince Kenneth said, "If I had not known it was the wrong place, we might have gone in to that house."

"This is bad," Lord Kenji said, "You would not be here if there everything is fine in the capital."

"We will explain the whole story if you would be willing to provide us with some food," Prince Kenneth said, "And perhaps afterwards a place to sleep."

"Of course," Lord Kenji said, "I was forgetting my manners. All of you come." Lord Kenji waved everyone inside, even the guards and the thief. The steward had already gone inside to let the cook know about the guests.

*"The grooms will come around and take care of your horses,"
Lord Kenji said, "Come in and rest and eat." The guards gave no
more thoughts about their horses before getting down to follow Lord
Kenji, Prince Kenneth, and Lord Jeggar. Mar hesitated briefly
before getting down from her wagon to be the last one in.*

Rana looked up at the sound of her name. Her maid
was standing there looking at her.

"Yes?" Rana asked.

"It is lunch time, Lady Rana," her maid answered.

"Or course," Rana said. She put her book in her
pocket before getting up to follow her maid into the
house. This day for lunch, Rana, her maid, Selwyn's wife
and Selwyn's daughter-in-law were the only ones eating
together as the men were all helping the workmen with
taking apart the left wing.

After lunch, Rana went back to her chair under the
tree. Her maid joined her after she had helped clean up.
Rana was still watching the men as they continued to take
down the walls of the left wing. Her maid started to sit
down and then got back to her feet.

"Lady Rana," her maid said, "Get up."

"What is it?" Rana asked as she got to her feet and
started toward her maid who was backing away from the
chairs.

Suddenly there was a loud crack and Rana looked. The
large branch over where Rana had been sitting had
broken and was dropping. She hurried to get farther away
as the branch came down. It crashed into the chair
causing it to break. But both Rana and her maid had been
far enough away to avoid being hit, even by the shrapnel
from the chair missing them.

Rana found herself shaking and her maid was not
much better. Duard and Havard came running.

"What happened?" Duard asked.

"The tree branch fell," Rana answered.

"Are you okay, Lady Rana?" Havard asked.

"Thanks to my maid, I am fine," Rana answered.

Duard stepped forward and examined the tree branch.

"I had not looked up and I think not think any of the branches were in danger of breaking," Rana said.

"Perhaps we should find another place for you to sit," Havard said as he led Rana and her maid away from the chairs. There was another set of chairs that were still in the shade of the trees, but there were no branches overhead. Rana sat and clasped her hands together to keep them from shaking. Her maid stayed beside her for support. Butterflies in Rana's stomach slowly settled down as she watched the guards cleaned up the branch. When the branch was chopped up into firewood, they put the chairs back together. When both chairs were ready, Duard climbed the tree to make sure no other branches were likely to come down anytime soon.

Rana was not comfortable moving back to the other chair, despite it looking very safe to do so. Her maid had to go inside after a while to do her chores. Duard sat down in the chair Rana's maid has been in. He did not say anything but merely sat there. Rana continued to watch the workmen, but she got tired and to keep herself awake she took out her book.

Lady Kenji was already seating in the dining room when everyone else entered. She rose to her feet when she saw that Prince Kenneth came in behind her husband.

"Welcome," Lady Kenji said with a curtsey.

"Thank you," Prince Kenneth replied.

"Come in, sit down," Lord Kenji said as he gestured to the chairs on the other side of the table from Lady Kenji, while he took

the chair at the end of the table. The company settled into their chairs as the steward brought in cups of cider for everyone.

"Food will be ready shortly," the steward reported before leaving again.

"What is going on?" Lady Kenji asked.

"They said they would tell us when they had a little time to rest," Lord Kenji answered.

"Of course," Lady Kenji said, "You must have come from the capital."

"Straight from the capital, Lady Kenji," Lord Jeggar said.

"Then you must be really tired," Lady Kenji said, "It must be something very serious that has brought you this far in a hurry."

"It is," Prince Kenneth said, "But we also come due to danger in your own backyard."

"Danger here?" Lady Kenji asked.

"Yes," Prince Kenneth answered, "A house that looks exactly like this one stands between here and the capital. We would have entered it, except it was too close to the village. However, we believe a messenger from the capital did not know about the distance, or was not paying attention and was diverted from his course to that house rather than coming here."

"That is very worrisome," Lord Kenji said, "Since we have not heard from anyone in four years the house could have been diverting people for a long time."

"Indeed," Prince Kenneth said, "We discussed going into see what it was about, but decided to come and rest before we tried."

"That is a good idea," Lord Kenji said, "When you return, I will go with you. I do not want people to confuse the houses any longer."

"But what is happening at the capital?" Lady Kenji asked.

"King Drax sent messengers out to gather his council because he was concerned about someone being after the crown," Prince Kenneth said, "And since none of the messengers came back and neither have any council members, the concern has grown."

"That is a serious concern," Lord Kenji said, "The person must be trying to prevent help from coming. We will of course pack up and head to the capital as soon as the phantom house has been dealt with."

"Should you not be at the capital?" Lady Kenji asked Prince Kenneth, "As the only heir being where you are most protected would make sense."

"No one is completely safe at the capital," Lord Jeggar said, "King Drax has been poisoned."

"What!" Lord Kenji asked.

"Someone poisoned King Drax using the jewel of Athum," Prince Kenneth replied, "Those in the capital are trying to sort out the hows and whos of the poisoning, while we are going in search of the leaves from the Kresk trees which should cure the poison."

"I guess that makes sense," Lord Kenji said.

"But the leaves are beyond the borders of the Dragon Shamus's territory," Lady Kenji said, "No one comes back alive from there."

"For the king's sake, we have to try," Prince Kenneth said, "But along the way we are stopping to see why members of the council did not get the messages or why they are not coming to the capital. This has been our first stop."

"If you are here, Lord Jeggar, who is at the capital to protect the king and figure who poisoned him?" Lord Kenji asked.

"Lord Sterling and Lord Fruend," Lord Jeggar answered.

"King Drax sent us with the message for Lord Sterling to come to council," Prince Kenneth said, "We were successful in getting to him and getting back. However, we were slowed down on the journey back goblins and a shade that had taken over Lord Fruend's tower."

"I have not heard anything from Lord Fruend in six years," Lord Kenji said, "I had not thought much about it because his family has always been infrequent in their visits anywhere, that was why he was not asked to be part of the council."

"His tower has been under control of a shade for the last six

years," Prince Kenneth said, "We managed to save him and get rid of the shade, but we came close to being stuck there ourselves."

"That is very concerning," Lord Kenji said, "Because if he was trapped for six years and the phantom house has been there for four years then the person has been working on this plan for a long time. They must know what is being done to counter their plans and be taking those measures against things."

"The last time anyone heard of the jewel of Athum, it was lost," Lady Kenji said, "There have been occasional speculation, but nothing proven. If this person has found the jewel of Athum then they have powerful resources."

"We are doing what we can," Prince Kenneth said, "The first step is to see how many of the council we can get to the capital and then get the antidote for King Drax. That is all we can do until we can figure out who is trying to take over the kingdom."

"Then to help we must feed you and let you rest so that you can look over the phantom house," Lady Kenji said. She was just about to get up and check what was keeping the food, but the steward arrived with plates for everyone. Once everyone had food, the steward topped up the cider in people's cups. Lord and Lady Kenji left the group alone to eat without worrying about conversation or more explanations.

Once the meal was finished, everyone was shown to a room that had been prepared for them. Mar turned down the use of the room and instead went to rest in her wagon. The steward was fine with that, but Prince Kenneth suspected that the steward was worried about stuff wandering off with Mar, though she had not stolen anything yet that he had noticed. But once in his room, all thoughts of the world vanished as he lay down on the bed and let sleep take him off to a place where he had no worries.

Mar sat against the wooden side of her wagon. The light came through each end of the cover over the wagon, but the canvas kept most of it out. She wanted to sleep and the light usually did not bother her. It probably was not the light keeping her awake. More likely it was the worry about the dreams returning. Mar scratched her wrist at those thoughts until she realized she was doing and stopped herself.

Every part of her being was urging her to hook up her horses and go the opposite direction from the dragon Shamus. However, Alim told Prince Kenneth that she would help get leaves from the Kresk tree. Mar owed Alim more than what this errand was worth. He usually did not remind her of them and he rarely asked her to do anything. This time Alim had been upset with her for taking the job to find the jewel of Athum and sell it to the court wizard of King Drax. King Drax had been friendly to Alim for many years. Even though Mar had tried to explain to Alim about money and having to take jobs as they came. She was not good enough to pick and choose her jobs as much as she really wanted.

The sound of someone coming into the stable reached Mar. She thought that it was strange because the grooms had just gone for supper. The horses started to become restless as if an intruder was in their presence. Mar moved a little so that she could see out the end of the wagon in hopes she could see whoever it was. At first she could not see anything moving, then it came into her line of sight. It wore the armour of the king's guards, but it lacked everything else except the shiny white bones that made up its skeleton.

Mar kept watching, but she did not move. The skeleton ignored the horses, though the horses seemed to want it to go away completely. It instead seemed to be following something else as it wandered the stable. It went right passed Mar's wagon and for a moment she could not see it until she moved to be able to look out the other side. The skeleton kept going. It wandered over to the stall of Prince Kenneth's horse. The horse was making noises like it was warning the skeleton away, but the skeleton paid it no notice as it stopped at the door to the stall.

The skeleton stayed there for a minutes as if trying to figure out what to do next. It moved its head around as if searching for the scent of something it could not quite get. The skeleton continued this behaviour for another several minutes. Then it caught whatever it was looking for and turned around. It went back the way it had come into the stable.

Mar slipped out of her wagon as quietly as she could and went to the exit the skeleton has used. She watched as it headed toward the house. One of the grooms was coming back from supper, but made no fuss at seeing the skeleton than if he had seen one of the king's guards. Mar figured that the skeleton must have an illusion around it and that is must have been sent from the phantom double of Lord Kenji's house. She was careful as she followed it across the lawn to Lord Kenji's house.

The thought that the skeleton was after Prince Kenneth or one of the party crossed Mar's mind as she followed, but she could not think of what giving things away this early would do for whomever was enchanting the house. To attack the prince or his traveling companions would certainly show the hand much too early. Thought they may not know about the plan to come visit the house after a rest, or they did hear about the rest and thought taking out Prince Kenneth in his sleep would be easier. It still did not make sense to Mar.

The skeleton stopped at the bottom step of the house. It tried to continue farther, but could not move. There was a magic barrier that the skeleton could not cross. Mar did not remember feeling anything when she went in, so it must be directed toward creatures such as the skeleton. Mar stayed out of sight, but wondered if she should step forward and deal with the skeleton. However before she could move, the steward came out of Lord Kenji's house with a sword in his hand.

The skeleton stood there as if he could not see the steward. It was still trying to get through the barrier. The steward stopped in front of the skeleton. He swung the sword, which cut through the skeleton and the armour. The skeleton collapsed to the ground like a puppet having just lost its strings. Lord Kenji came out of the *house to join the steward in removing the skeleton from where it had fallen.*

Mar waited until they were out of sight before going back to the stable. The groom was nowhere in sight, but she could hear someone shoveling. She got back into her wagon and lay down on her bed. She may not know what the future had in store, but this was a safe place to sleep for now.

Duard moved causing Rana to look up from her book. Her maid was coming out of the house and toward them, which was what caused Duard to get to his feet. Rana figured this was the call for supper so she put her book away and got to her feet. She followed Duard and her maid inside to the dining room.

After supper, Rana went to her room. The workmen had gone for the day shortly before supper, but Selwyn and some of the other men who were living at the house kept working on taking apart the left wing. With Rana in her room, Duard could go back to helping because she was sure he figured that she was safe in her room. The noise was faint, so it did not bother her as she went back to reading her book.

Prince Kenneth went back to the dining room after he has woken up and was ready to go. He found Lord Kenji and Lord Jeggar were already there. Prince Kenneth sat down in a chair near them.

"When everyone is awake supper should be ready," Lord Kenji said, "And there should be enough light left in the day for us to check out the phantom house."

"Good," Prince Kenneth said, "Did anything happen?"

"A skeleton showed up," Lord Kenji answered, "It appeared to have followed you, though we cannot be sure who in specific it was following. My steward dealt with it as he has had plenty of

experience with that sort of thing since his father taught him about it. I hired him on because of that experience after finding out that there are several grave yards in this area and the graves are found to be dug up with regularity."

"Is this the first time a skeleton come?" Prince Kenneth asked.

"No, but most of them have not had that level of focus," Lord Kenji answered, "Most appear to be mistakes that the caster has ignored. This one also was wearing King Drax's armour."

"It could have been the messenger sent for you," Lord Jeggar said.

"It could have been," Lord Kenji said, "I would wish the soul a better death, but it is possible."

"So, it could be a necromancer who has set up the phantom house," Prince Kenneth said.

"I did not think that was possible," Lord Jeggar said, "King Drax's father outlawed those magics and had the kingdom spelled against such people gaining power."

"If people can raise skeletons at random and leave them wandering than the spell is not as strong here," Prince Kenneth said.

"The thief said that it would take a powerful wizard to cast such an illusion spell," Lord Jeggar said.

"She also said it could be a powerful spell," Prince Kenneth said, "And illusion spells are not necessarily part of necromancy. They are used by all sorts of spell casters. So, the necromancer does not have to be strong if the spell is."

"Does it not take a strong wizard to cast a strong spell?" Lord Jeggar asked.

"It depends on how and where they gather their energy," Lord Kenji answered, "Most spell casters use their own energy so they either have to have a lot to start with or time to recharge. But if it is a necromancer, the energy could be coming from almost anywhere. He could be draining another being of energy to fuel his spell."

"Horrifying," Lord Jeggar said.

"And a good reason to stop the necromancer before he does any more damage," Prince Kenneth said.

The thief stepped in to the doorway of the dining room. She acted as if she had not heard any of the discussion, but Prince Kenneth was sure she had heard most of it. The thief took a seat a little way down the table from the men.

"Supper will arrive when everyone else has gotten up," Lord Kenji said, *"I hope you had a restful sleep."*

"As much as I usually do," the thief said, *"I am sorry if I interrupted anything."*

"It was pretty much the end of the discussion anyway," Lord Kenji said, *"Lord Jeggar says you were traveling with Alim, how did you meet him?"*

"We were both traveling in the same direction and I stopped him from running into an ambush," the thief answered, *"After that if I needed someone to travel with and he was heading in the same direction, he allowed me to travel with him."*

"It must be nice to have such a friend," Lord Kenji said.

"Almost as nice as having someone with necromancy knowledge on the payroll," the thief replied.

"You saw the guard?" Lord Kenji asked.

"Not as you did," the thief answered, *"Though most guards still have skin and muscle among other such normal things."*

"You could see the skeleton?" Lord Kenji asked.

"As a thief, it is hard to steal illusions," The thief said, *"So, the ability to see through them is very useful."*

"Then you will be helpful getting through a phantom house," Lord Kenji said.

"I am not particularly interested in crossing into that place," the thief replied, *"I will go and wait along the road in case you need rescuing, but if I do not have to go inside I will not."*

"Understandable," Lord Kenji said.

"You do not have to follow us inside," Prince Kenneth said, *"You can wait at the road and only come after us if we run into*

trouble."

Lord Jeggar looked about to argue, but something must have stopped him because he did not speak up. Mar nodded, but did not say anything else. The whole conversation changed again because two of the guards came into the dining room.

Lord Kenji finally had the steward wake the last two guards when it seemed as though they would not get up on their own within the time everyone hoped to have eaten and left.

After the meal was over, Prince Kenneth went back to the room and gathered his belongings. It did not take him long before he was headed out to the front steps of Lord Keji's house. Lord Jeggar was already waiting along with the grooms who were holding the horses. Prince Kenneth took his horse from the groom and mounted.

"The rest should be here shortly," Lord Jeggar said, "But I am not sure where the thief went."

"I would assume that she knows enough to join us when she is ready," Prince Kenneth said, "Since she was sitting there when we discussed the plan."

Lord Jeggar did not say anything, merely nodded.

"She is along for a reason," Prince Kenneth said, "And she done her part."

"I just do not trust her," Lord Jeggar said.

"You do not have to trust her," Prince Kenneth said, "You just have to accept that she is part of this company."

Before Lord Jeggar could respond, the sounds of horses' hoofs and wheels on the cobblestones reached them. Both men looked in toward where the sound was coming from and saw the thief driving her wagon to the meeting place. She maneuvered her wagon to a space where it would be easy for her to follow the horses out the gates and then she stopped to wait.

The guards came out of Lord Kenji's house and got ready to go. That left only one horse without a rider. One groom stayed to hold that horse while the rest headed back to the stable. The party waited without talking. Prince Kenneth saw Lord Jeggar check where the sun was and how much time they had until sundown.

The door opened and Lady Kenji stepped out. She looked at the travelers and frowned at the riderless horse. Before she could go back inside to make inquiries the steward stepped outside. Prince Kenneth could not hear Lady Kenji's question, but he was sure that she was asking Lord Kenji's location. The steward's answer was short and obviously reassured Lady Kenji.

A moment later Lord Kenji came out of the house with his bag. He kissed his wife before climbing up on his horse.

"Sorry to keep you waiting," Lord Kenji said as he got settled.

"It is fine," Prince Kenneth said, "Everyone ready?"

The men of the group replied in the affirmative. Prince Kenneth glanced back at the thief, but she just shrugged. Prince Kenneth turned back to the front and started for the gate. Everyone else followed him. Lady Kenji and the steward waved from the steps.

The twenty minute ride back to the double of Lord Kenji's house was quiet. Prince Kenneth found his thoughts going back to the talk of a skeleton which had been seen at Lord Kenji's house during the time the group had been resting. Who was the person controlling the skeleton? And why send it to Lord Kenji's house? Was there a particular target?

Once again the group stopped in front of the house that looked exactly like Lord Kenji's house. Prince Kenneth studied the house, but could not see any difference between this building and Lord Kenji's house. Then he noticed one tree near the stable which was not present on the other property. It was a tall tree with branches starting half way up and full of leaves. Prince Kenneth thought it had been pruned.

Prince Kenneth was finished his check and was about to suggest they go forward when he noticed that Lord Kenji was still staring at the house. His face was a mixture of wonder and outrage. Prince Kenneth understood Lord Kenji's reaction, but knew it was best for everyone to keep calm.

"Shall we dismount and find out what is going on with this house?" Prince Kenneth asked. Lord Kenji came out of his own thoughts to look at Prince Kenneth. Once the question sunk in, Lord Kenji shut down the emotions and he nodded.

The party dismounted and tied the reins of their horses to the thief's wagon. The thief stayed in the driver's seat of the wagon. Prince Kenneth noticed that Mar was not looking at the house and he wondered about it. Could the thief see the house at all? She had told Lord Kenji that she could see through illusions, so she might know what they were walking in to and was going to wait on her wagon. But he had said that it was okay, so he would not change this mind.

The men gathered in front of the gate and waited for Prince Kenneth to be ready. He pushed the gate open. It felt real enough, as did the cobblestones of the drive as he led the group toward the house. The main difference that Prince Kenneth noticed as they got closer was that there was no people. No one came out of the house to greet them and no grooms came out of the stable to see if there were any horses.

Prince Kenneth led the party up the stairs into the house. The door opened as if it was real and Prince Kenneth thought it felt real too. The interior looked exactly like the interior of Lord Kenji's house and Prince Kenneth could not see any differences. The group split into two and went to either side of the entry hall. Prince Kenneth went to the right followed by Lord Kenji and one of the guards. Lord Jeggar and the rest of the guards went to the left.

The mens did not run into anything they could not see and there still was no one coming out to greet them. Either there was no one here or it was an ambush. Prince Kenneth took out his sword as he continued forward. The guardsman did the same but Lord Kenji left his sword sheathed.

They got close to the end of the entry hall to where there was a door off to each side and one at the end. Prince Kenneth moved toward the door on the right. Lord Kenji and the guardsman followed him. Before they got too close there was a short yell from Lord Jeggar. Prince Kenneth looked over. Lord Jeggar and the guardsmen were being attacked by skeletons that were coming through the door on the left side. Prince Kenneth turned back to the door on his side just in time to see skeletons coming through the door beside them. He brought up his sword to defend against the skeleton's attack. Lord Kenji pulled out his sword, but was a full second too late. The next skeleton was swinging a club and hit Lord Kenji in the side of the head. This caused Lord Kenji to collapse to the floor and not get back up. Prince Kenneth found himself caught up in fighting the group of skeletons that were coming at him that he could not tend Lord Kenji. The guardsman was in the same position.

With too many enemies in front of him, Prince Kenneth found himself backing up. Rather than surround him, the skeletons let him and the guardsman go backwards. But they were not being backed toward the door; instead they were being backed toward Lord Jegger and the guards with him which was being forced to do the same thing. Prince Kenneth did not know what to do aside from continuing to back up. There were too many skeletons coming at him and he was doing very little damage to the ones he was hitting with his sword. The two groups were getting close to the middle of the entry hall and soon be back to back.

Prince Kenneth took another step back and instead of ending up back to back with Lord Jeggar and the other guardsmen, he fell. As did the guardsman fighting with him and the others from the other side of the entry hall. They fell about ten feet into a very narrow trench. After the shock of the fall, Prince Kenneth prepared for the skeletons to follow them. However, the skeletons stayed up top and then disappeared from sight. Everyone stayed still for another minute before checking if anything was broken.

Since he did not feel any place throbbing more than other part, Prince Kenneth was sure that nothing was broken and got to his feet. He sheathed his sword before looking around. The trench appeared to run the length of the house with some lumps at the end closest to the door. As everyone else was getting to their feet and dusting themselves off, Prince Kenneth wandered down the trench. One of the guardsmen, who had also gotten to his feet fairly quickly followed him.

They found that the lumps were a handful of men who had stepped into the trench and expected to find a floor. None of them seemed to have survived, though it appeared to be starvation and dehydration that killed them not necessarily the fall. At least one was wearing the royal crest.

"This seems to be what has happened the messenger," the guardsman said.

"And we would have fallen sooner had we not split up at the door," Prince Kenneth said, "It looks almost like whoever is doing this does not care about taking prisoners, or who falls in as long as they do not get any farther than the trench."

"I have seen a trench similar to this before," the guardsman said studying the walls and floor.

"Where?" Prince Kenneth asked.

"I cannot remember," the guardsman answered, "But it looks very familiar."

"When you remember tell me," Prince Kenneth said, "Any information is going to aid our rescue."

Prince Kenneth headed back to where the rest were gathered with the guardsman wandering behind him.

The company was trying to figure out what to do next when suddenly something fell from above. It landed with a thud and did not move. Lord Jeggar moved to check it out.

"It is Lord Kenji," Lord Jeggar said, "And he does not appear to be hurt aside from an injury to the head."

"He was knocked out before we were pushed back into this trench," Prince Kenneth said, "Is he alive?"

"He is breathing," Lord Jeggar said.

"Good," Prince Kenneth said, "While we wait for him to wake

up, we need to find a way out of here."

"The wall is only ten feet," the nearest guardsman said, "And made up of dirt. It should not be difficult to climb up."

"Might as well try it," Prince Kenneth said, "But one at a time, so that we can help out in case of any issues."

"Here is a good place to start," Lord Jeggar pointed to the wall in front of them.

Prince Kenneth stepped back and let the guardsman go first. Lord Jeggar and the other guardsmen helped him make hands and footholds before lifting him. Prince Kenneth and the other guardsman moved Lord Kenji away from where they were working and to a place where he could be somewhat comfortable. The guardsman got up to the top of the wall and it looked like he might get out when a skeleton appeared at the top to knock him back into the trench. The guardsman managed not to injure himself when he fell. The skeleton stepped back out of sight.

"We cannot go up this way," Lord Jeggar said, "Those skeleton seem to be there to make sure we stay down here."

"If we do not find some way to get out of here we are going to run into the same problem as the others at the end of the trench," the guardsman near Prince Kenneth said.

"I do not think we will be here that long," Prince Kenneth said.

"And what is the thief going to do?" Lord Jeggar asked.

"I do not know," Prince Kenneth answered, "But she claimed the ability to see through illusions and she is out there. If she cannot help us, hopefully she will go back to Lord Kenji's house and get help from Lord Kenji's steward."

"We can hope she is smart enough to go back to get Lord Kenji's steward," Lord Jeggar said as he found himself a place to sit. Prince Kenneth kept the sigh in as he too found someplace to sit in the dirt on the bottom of the trench.

The book fell to the floor as Rana could not keep her eyes open. Sleep was there welcoming her in and she was embracing it. It was a lovely place to be. Creak..creak… creak..creak, creak, creak. Rana groaned as she came out of the pleasantness which she had been sinking. She got up, put the book on the table, and then got ready for bed. When she was ready, Rana climbed into bed and hoped sleep would come as easily there as it had in the chair.

Rana found herself lying in bed as the sun peaked over the horizon. Sleep have gone away far too early and Rana wanted it to come back. Instead, she was lying there and hoping her stomach would not decide to leave her as it was threatening. Her muscles were starting to twitch as if she was not going to stay still much longer. Finally, Rana got out of bed. She did it slowly so as not to bother her stomach.

Since her maid was not up yet, Rana got her own clothing to get dressed in. When she went to leave her room, Rana found Havard standing guard.

"Good morning," Rana said.

"Good morning," Havard replied.

"Is there some reason I am in danger?" Rana asked.

"Duard and I are not sure," Havard answered, "But that branch did not break on its own. It was cut."

"Thank you for watching out for me," Rana said, "I appreciate it. I cannot sleep, so I was going to take a walk outside."

"I will go with you," Havard said.

"Of course," Rana said. She started down the hallway. Havard let her get several steps ahead of him before falling in behind her. It was enough to give her some privacy while still being close enough to help her should she need it.

Rana went out the front door and wandered in the chilly dawn air. There was dew on everything to glitter in the sunshine. It was calm and Rana found it relaxing. Her stomach settled down and she wondered if she could sleep if she sat down in the chair. She did not sit down though because the chairs were wet.

Out of curiosity, Rana wandered over to the work area. They had done a lot more work than Rana had thought they would. The foreman had suggested they would get at least that much done. There was plenty of time to get it all done. She was not planning to move back to the castle anytime soon, so this was going to be her home from now on.

Rana took another step forward to look at something, which caught her attention. Havard was checking on something else at a slight distance from her. There was a cracking sound and then suddenly the floor gave way causing Rana to fall into a hole. She fell about ten feet before a dirt floor stopped her. She had cried out at the suddenness of the drop, but the jarring at the bottom caused her to stop. Her breath had been taken out of her.

Sitting there, she managed to get her breath back and looked around. It appeared to be a cellar that had been covered over and forgotten. It was all packed dirt with nothing else aside from the debris which had come with Rana. There was some dust in the air, which cause Rana to cough a couple times.

"Lady Rana!" Havard's voice came from above her.

"I am okay," Rana replied, "I think." She tried to get to her feet but found pain shot through her ankle.

"My ankle hurts," Rana said, "But otherwise I seem to be okay."

"I will go get some help," Havard said.

"Good idea," Rana said. She did not try to move again and instead sat back.

It was several minutes before she could hear people

above her. Some ropes were lower and then Havard came down the side. He helped Rana to her feet before making a seat around her with the rope. Then he called up and with everyone's help Rana was taken out of the hole. When she was on top, Duard untied her. Selwyn's wife was there to help her limp back into the house.

Rana sat in the chair in the kitchen as Selwyn's daughter-in-law wrapped her ankle. Then Selwyn came into the kitchen.

"I am sorry about what happened," Selwyn said.

"I hardly think you were to blame for the incident," Rana said.

"The hole was not there yesterday when we were taking down walls," Selwyn said, "I do not know what happened."

"I am fine," Rana said, "As long as the hole gets filled in and everyone is careful from now on, there is no problem."

Selwyn hesitated for a moment before nodding and leaving the kitchen. Havard came into the kitchen as Rana tried to get to her feet. He had a crutch, which he offered to Rana. She accepted it and used it to go into the dining room so as to leave others to finish cooking breakfast.

In the dining room, Rana sat down in the chair. Havard sat down as well. He did not seem to need to apologize for the incident, nor ask what exactly happened.

"Selwyn said there was no hole yesterday," Rana said.

"He is right," Havard replied, "The ground underneath that part of the building had no such holes in it. This place has no cellars under the building."

"Then someone would have to have dug it overnight," Rana said, "And no one would have known I would be wandering through the construction area."

"It is still better that you are careful than for anything

serious to happen to you," Havard said, "You need to be extra careful from now on."

"I will be much more alert from now on," Rana said, "I will also try to stay away from any place I might be in danger."

"And Duard or I will also be around to keep an eye out," Havard said.

"Then I should be okay," Rana said, "This morning I was going to sit outside and read. This afternoon I was going to do some work at the desk in my room."

"Duard will sit with you outside after breakfast," Havard said, "And I will guard outside your room this afternoon. If you find yourself in danger this afternoon, all you will have to do it call for help."

"Okay," Rana said, "Thank you."

"You are welcome, Lady Rana," Havard said.

Selwyn's daughter-in-law at that moment brought in the plates to set the table and they did not say anything more to each other.

As she planned, Rana went outside after breakfast. She used the crutch to go over to the chair, which was not directly under a tree. She felt safer there. The workmen were already busy. Their first job of the morning likely had been to fill in the hole and then they would have been able to continue on where they had left off from the day before.

Duard came out and sat down in the other chair. He did not say anything but kept a watch on everything going on. Rana left him to it as she opened her book and started to read.

Mar watched as the sun touched the horizon. The men had not come back yet, but she hardly expected them to have made it back.

None of them could see through the illusions they claimed made the house look like Lord Kenji's house. She could not see any houses on the property to which they kept referring to as the duplicate house, instead she saw a country church surrounded by a graveyard. Most of the graves had been dug up leaving gaping holes. Mar thought that the men might fall into one of these graves, but they managed to avoid them on the way into the church.

Once they had gone into the church, Mar could no longer see them or what was happening to them as the door had closed behind them. However, she thought she had seen some skeletons briefly in the light that had come in through the holes in the roof. That would suggest that the men had run into skeletons, which should have killed them by now. Except that Mar knew that the men were still alive.

Mar sighed as she got off the wagon. This time she would have to rescue them without the help of Isadora. Her horse stayed exactly where it was and would not move until she climbed back up on to the driver's seat. She walked across the road and entered the gate the men had left open. Mar did not head into the church as the men did because she figured that it had to be a trap. Instead she started walking around the graves to the left side of the church. There was a large tree, which looked to be tended and most creatures did not bother with taking care of trees. Most creatures would either destroy the tree or leave it alone.

Not all the graves were dug up, but the ones that were had headstones which looked older. Any of the newer headstones had graves left undisturbed. Mar remembered someone once telling her about the fact that the older the grave the easier it was for a necromancer to control the body, which made skeletons easier to animate than zombies. So, whoever was doing this preferred corpses that were easier to control.

The sun had gone down and there was no light from it left, but the moon was partially full and gave Mar plenty of light to avoid open graves as well as see the circumstances. She reached the tree, but there was nothing around it to help her. However from there she could see a small, rough building resting against the back of the church. It appeared to be scrap pieces of wood nailed together into two walls and a roof.

Mar moved quietly toward it. She could not hear anything coming from inside until she was fairly close to the building. Someone inside was laughing and talking to themselves.

"You will never get out of my prison," the voice had a whiny quality to it, "You will suffer in the worst way possible. My pawns will guard you and knock you down every time you try to escape. My plan is working so well. Nothing can stop me now." This last statement brought out laughter in the person.

Mar peeked through a gap in the boards. There was a candle sitting on a rickety table along with a mirror showing a trench with figures sitting in the bottom.

There was yelling from the workmen causing Rana to be interrupted in her reading. She looked up at them and saw they were all gathering around an area. Duard was watching them with interest. Using the crutch to get to her feet, Rana left the book on her chair as she headed over to see what was going on. Duard followed her.

They found the workmen were all gathered around a piece of flooring on which was painted magical symbols. There was nervousness among the men and some muttering. Rana studied the symbols for several minutes.

"Cut around them," Rana told the foreman.

"What?" the foreman asked looking at her.

"Cut around them," Rana said, "You cannot burn them where they are without burning the rest of the building down. So cut them out and burn them in a space separate from the building."

"Okay," the foreman said with a nod, "You all heard her, cut them out."

The men did not hesitate at following the foreman's directions. Rana used her crutch to go over to where there was a fire pit behind the building. Duard brought over the stuff she needed and she started a fire in the fire pit. It did not take long before she had a good little fire going. Rana added more wood to make it bigger. By the time the men brought over the wood pieces with the magical symbols on them, the fire was plenty big enough to just toss the piece in. There was a flash of red light as the fire burned the wood, but then it just burned like all the rest of the logs in the fire pit.

Rana stayed near the fire pit as the piece of wood was burned to ash and then she continued to stay there as the fire burned down. Most of the morning went by as she stood there and watched the fire burn. It did slowly burn to down to ash. It was still smoking when Rana's maid came out to call Rana and Duard for lunch. Rana did not immediately head inside but instead went back to her chair to get her book.

Except her book was not there. Rana looked under the chair and around it, but the book was gone. Rana was highly disappointed, but she was not sure what else to do besides go inside for lunch.

After lunch, Rana headed up to her room with her maid and Havard following her. She went inside her room. Her maid followed her inside, but Havard took up his position outside the door. Rana sat down at the desk with paper and ink while her maid did some clean up. Despite knowing what she should say, Rana was having trouble putting any words down on paper. Eventually, her maid finished with the cleaning and left the room. Now Rana got up and used the crutch to go to the window. She looked out but did not see any of what was out there.

Her mind spun on what to say in a letter to her brother. Finally, she thought she might know what she was going to say. Rana sat back down and put her pen to the paper.

Dear Weldon,

I arrived at the country estate safely. There were no incidents along the way. I felt much safer the farther away from Hillel I got. It is a relief to arrive here and have something to take my mind off everything I left behind. I am renovating the house at the country estate. The steward is helping me and very much agreed with me about the house needing the work as well as how I wanted to change things. Right now the workmen are tearing down the left wing of the house, which once it is done they will start rebuilding. The main part of the house just requires some basic fixes so they will not have to take it completely down and rebuild it. The right wing will need some tearing down, but not the whole thing. I figure it would be a good idea to do things in stages so each piece can be completely finished before the next one is started. And as I said the steward agrees with me.

I hope you are doing well. I know it is hard to direct Hillel, but I have faith that you are the best person for the job. I hope everything else is going well there at the castle. I have found it very peaceful and calming out here as oppose to being there. There are a lot fewer people making it a much quieter place to be. I may start to go crazy for lack of things happening, but I think it might take a while for that to happen.

There have been a few disturbing incidents since the work has started on the left wing of the house. A branch just about landed on me and instead destroyed the chair I had been sitting in. My maid saw it and warned me in time. Also, a hole was dug overnight in the area of the construction and in my wandering this morning I managed to be the one to stumble over it. I am okay, but my ankle is a little sore. The last thing that happened was the men found a piece of flooring which had magical symbols on it. I had them burn it, but I hope it does not prevent any of the men from coming back to work tomorrow. Some places are very uncertain about magic.

Since these things have happened, the guards have been keeping a closer watch on me. I go back and forth in thoughts between these are directed at me and being very grateful the guards are here. They will keep me as safe as they can while still giving me room to live. I hope there are no other worrying incidents, but even if there are I am not worried about my safety.

I will write you again as soon as anything interesting happens. I hope to hear from you if there is anything you need help with.

Your sister, Rana

Rana waited a moment for the letter to dry before folding it up and tucking it into the envelope. She put her brother's name on the envelope before sealing it. Then Rana took the letter to Selwyn to get him to send it off as soon as possible. Then she went to where the library was being stored. She found a couple books that looked interesting to take back to her room, which was where she spent the rest of the afternoon. One of the books was titled The Secrets of Marriage and that was the one Rana chose to read first.

EUSTACE RETURNS AND THE SITUATION BECOMES CLEAR

Rana decided to spend the evening in her room as usual because it was much easier for her guards. She went back to reading the books she had borrowed from the library but missed The Prince and the Rogue as she really wanted to know how it would end. Rana sat in the chair and tried to concentrate on the book.

She had let the book lower to her lap and was staring into space when there was a scratching at the window. Rana glanced nervously at the window, but could not see whatever was making the noise. She put the book down and went over to the window. Looking out, Rana saw something white without being able to see exactly what it was. She opened the window. Once there was enough room, Eustace slipped in. He held a crystal in his claws. Eustace set down on the table while Rana closed the window.

"Where have you been?" Rana asked as she sat down in the chair.

Eustace's response was to nudge the crystal closer to Rana. Unsure, Rana picked up the crystal and placed it in her hand. It warmed quickly to her touch.

"What is it?" Rana asked as she studied it. Eustace did not say anything but sat back. The crystal was clear with four coloured spirals inside and a smooth surface. Heat from her hand continued to warm up the crystal. Slowly the smooth area grew cloudy and a face started to appear in it. At first, Rana could not tell who it was and then it came into focus. The face was that of Luce.

"Luce?" Rana asked.

"Oh good," the image replied in Luce's voice, "Eustace got back to you with the communication crystal."

"Is that what this is?" Rana asked.

"Yes," Luce answered, "It lets us talk to each other over long distances. It does require some warming up first, but it usually does not take long. I would have sent the stand to go with the crystal, but Eustace had enough trouble with the crystal. I will find some other way to send the stand to you because if the conversation is too long the crystal can get really hot."

"Why?" Rana asked.

"Eustace showed up and gave every indication that you were in trouble," Luce answered, "I wish I could drop everything to help you, but I got myself into a little bit of a situation which is going to take time to get out. So, I thought it might be best to send the communication crystal and then we can talk about anything that might be going on. I am not sure what other help I can provide."

"I am not sure about being in trouble," Rana said, "But there have been some strange incidents since I came out to the country estate."

"What kind of strange incidents?" Luce asked.

"Cut tree branches, holes dug overnight, and magic symbols showing up on pieces of flooring," Rana said, "I twisted my ankle, but am otherwise fine. They all just seem strange."

"It sounds like you have trouble there," Luce said, "I would suggest you keep an eye out for more strange happenings."

"I am," Rana said, "Along with both guards who came with me."

"Until something further happens, which points to a more specific source, I am not sure I can be of any help."

"Well, it is nice to talk to you," Rana said.

"Why did you decide to move out the country estate?" Luce said, "I thought you liked living at the castle."

"I thought it might be a good idea to get away from Hillel," Rana said, "Something about him makes me nervous. Weldon and I were given a country estate just in case we wanted to get away from the castle. He said I could have it if he could use the house in the city as his residence. I agreed to it and now I am making the country estate livable."

"Something to keep you busy as well as get you away from Hillel," Luce said, "That makes sense. I hope you are not in trouble there."

"I do not think so, but the guards are not taking any chances," Rana said, "I should be okay and now with this crystal if anything more happens I can let you know. Then you can tell me if you think it is anything to worry about."

"Okay," Luce said with a laugh, "I will look forward to hearing from you. All you have to do is warm up the crystal."

"Thank you," Rana said, "Good-bye."

"Good-bye," Luce said and then he was gone. Rana set the crystal on the table and stared at it for a minute. It was long enough for Eustace to crawl into her lap and butt her hand with his head. She scratched him behind the ears in response.

"So, that is where you got to," Rana said, "I wondered where you went. I am not sure about the trouble. It could very well be true, but I am not certain. Anyway, I think it might be time to turn in for the night." She set Eustace back down on the table before getting changed into her nightgown.

Rana then crawled into bed. Eustace flew over and curled up on the pillow beside her.

"Good night," Rana whispered. Eustace grunted with his usual affection. Rana closed her eyes and tried to relax, but visions of Luce stayed with her. She pushed them away and focused on getting to sleep. As she got closer to being a sleep, Rana heard the creaking start from the floor below. This time instead of feeling annoyed, she just felt lonely.

After breakfast the next morning, the workers showed up at their usual time. Rana had brought one of the books out to read outside. Duard had taken up the other chair. Eustace was curled up in the grass in a sunny spot. It was quiet even with the sound of the workmen. Rana was still having trouble concentrating on the new book as her mind wanted to finish the other one. Sometimes her mind would think about Luce for a while, but she tried not to let her emotions get too connected to her thoughts. It was best to view him in his concern for her safety then with connection with the new life in her stomach. The one no one knew about. The one who survived the fall of ten feet, something she was extremely grateful for. If she lost her child, Rana was not sure there was much point in living.

Several of the workers went passed the chairs with stuff they had removed from the left wing and was piling in another area of the lawn. The pile had been building over the last couple days. This was usual and had not bothered Rana or whichever guard was sitting with her. However as the group of men got closer Eustace curled himself and growled at the men. Rana and Duard looked up at Eustace while the men looked over from their work. Eustace was bristling and distressed with something, but Rana could not figure out what. Her dragon backed toward her as if to protect her from the men. The men stared at the dragon for a few minutes as they had never seen a dragon before. No one came closer as Eustace was not happy about their presence. Finally, the men shrugged and continued on with their work. They dropped the stuff in the pile before going back to the left wing of the house. Only once they men were back at the normal distance did Eustace calm down and curled back up to relax in the sun.

"Has he done such things before?" Duard asked.

"I have never seen such behaviour from him," Rana answered.

"Perhaps he thinks the workmen are a danger to you," Duard said.

"He could think that," Rana said, "But they do not come near me so I would not think they were any danger to me."

"It is something to watch anyway," Duard said.

"I suppose so," Rana said. Duard did not say anything else, so Rana went back to her book.

She did notice when another workman went passed

with more stuff for the pile and Eustace did not move from his spot. He did not even look up at the man, but instead kept enjoying his sleep. Duard watched this behaviour even as Rana noted it. None of the other workmen came passed for a while as they were busy with something else for a long while and did not need to put anything in the pile.

Rana was starting to actually concentrate on her book and get into the story. She might have been kept in if she had not heard the warning growl from Eustace. Rana looked up to see a single workman going passed with more stuff for the pile. Eustace was not happy with the man's presence. The workman ignored the dragon and continued on with his work just as any of the rest of them would have done.

Once the workman went back to work on the left wing, Eustace settled down again to relax in the sun. Rana kept an eye on the man over her book. He looked like all the other workmen with his brown hair, solid frame, and brown clothes. There was nothing to set him apart from any of the other workmen, except Eustace's reaction to him. Rana was not quite sure what that meant, but she needed to keep that workman away from her. Eustace would make sure of some of it. Rana noticed Duard had also checked out the workman and any danger he might be to Rana. She went back to her book and was glad about both her security systems.

At lunch, she went inside with Duard and Eustace. For the afternoon, Rana spent it in her room with Havard standing guard outside and Eustace curled up in her lap. Rana felt she could relax with such guards, which caused her to put her book down and fall asleep in the chair.

About the middle of the evening, Rana picked up the

communication crystal Eustace brought her and set it in the middle of her hand. She gave it time to warm up. Slowly the smooth part clouded over and Luce appeared.

"Did something happen?" Luce asked. He was still pretty blurry, but she could still recognize him.

"Eustace reacted to one of the workmen," Rana answered, "I was trying to figure out what that means. I know he tends to growl when I am in danger, but the workman has done nothing more than the rest of the workmen."

"Eustace is most likely reacting to the man because of something you cannot see," Luce said, "There is something magical about the man, which Eustace does not like. Sometimes that means the man is a demon who is disguised as a human. Use Eustace's judgement and keep your distance."

"But if all the incidents have been small things, which appear to have no connection than he could cause a lot more trouble and people may get hurt," Rana said, "If the man is a demon, is there some way to tell? Because if he is a demon, he needs to be removed from the situation."

"Sometimes the only way to tell if someone is a demon is to get them to reveal themselves," Luce said, "Other times you can use a magical item to see through the disguise. There is also a herb mixture, which helps a person see through magical illusions that someone might employ."

"What does the herb mixture take?" Rana asked as she picked up a pen and paper from the table, "That sounds like the best solution for this situation."

"Three clover, a handful of sage, dandylion head, a twig from a rose bush, and a handful of leaves from a bean vine," Luce said, "You put them in a pot of water and boil it for half an hour. Then you have to leave it to cool completely before you drink it. However, you have to use it the day you make because it loses its potency."

"Okay," Rana said, "I will have to try it tomorrow and see if it can help me see whether the workman is a demon in disguise."

"What will you do if he is a demon?" Luce asked.

"I do not know," Rana answered, "What does one usually do with a demon?"

"Most of us learn what we can about the demon through books on the subject," Luce said, "Because it teaches us about the demon's weakness and how to kill it. Some demons have to be killed in specific ways or it does not work."

"Where do I find a book on demons?" Rana asked.

"I know there is one in the king's study in the castle, but I am not sure where else you might find one," Luce said, "Perhaps you can just make notes as to what the demon looks like and then give me the description. I can look it up and give you what information you need. Then you can get your guards to help deal with the demon."

"They will have to help with the demon," Rana said, "I very much doubt I could deal with this demon on my own."

"As much as I would come and help, I cannot," Luce said, "There is not even anything I can send to help you. However, if I stumble across anything that might protect you, I will send it along."

"Thank you," Rana said, "I appreciate all the help."

"Keep Eustace close to you," Luce said.

"He has not left my side since he got back," Rana said, "I do not think he would leave if I told him to."

"He would, but only if there was a good reason," Luce said, "He is your dragon and that includes taking orders from you."

"I do not order him to do anything," Rana said, "I leave the choice up to him, it is better that way."

"Well, keep him near you and be careful," Luce said, "The herb mixture should work for seeing the demon and provide you with a good description for me."

"Okay," Rana said, "I will talk to you again tomorrow about the same time."

"I will answer when you call," Luce said before disappearing. Rana put the communication crystal back on the table. Eustace brushed against Rana's hand. She scratched behind his ears just as he wanted.

Rana did not bother to pick up the book again. The story was somewhat boring as it was the story of a widow, who was being blackmailed into marrying the town bully because he found out that she had someone kill her husband. Rana wondered if she would have someone kill the bully and save herself from the horror of the marriage, but so far the widow seemed to be giving in without any fight. Instead, there were paragraphs of her bemoaning her fate. There was still plenty of book left for her to figure out how to kill the bully, but with the recent arrival of another man, who after seeing him once now haunted the widow's dreams, suggested that someone else was going to take care of the bully for her. Rana did not think the widow needed help solving the issue, but she supposed that if the widow did things the way Rana thought she should the book would be much shorter. It might even be taken down to a short story. But the book also had not explained why the widow had had her husband killed in the first place and how she was a victim for having done it.

Instead, Rana sat there and thought about Luce. She missed him a lot, but she had known he would not stay anywhere. But she wondered why he was helping her. Did he actually care about her? He claimed he could not come help her because he could not get out of his current situation. Was there a woman involved in that situation? Would she be jealous if there was? She had never thought of Luce as being hers in any way except as her lover for a brief time. If he chose to take another lover, it was none of her business. After all, she had not told him about the child who was coming. She saw it as the child being hers and not theirs. With such thinking, did it matter if he moved on from their relationship?

Was there really a demon among the workmen? Or was Eustace responding to something else? Was he likely to respond to anything else? She knew someone was causing the incidents. Rana was not sure she was the target, except that with the branch because that was right above the chair she had been sitting in by habit. But no one could have known she was going to walk around the construction area to fall into the hole. Anyone could have done that. In fact, she probably should not have been in the construction area at all, which made the hole a trap for someone else. And no one knew what the magical symbols meant, so they could have been there to bless the place by the last person to do construction work on the left wing.

However, with the guards' concern and Eustace's response to things, Rana had trouble convincing herself that the incidents were just coincidence and she could not be the target. Something in her gut suggested, despite logic to the otherwise, she was the specific target of a demon.

Rana remembered what Luce said about the information about demons being in books. She got to her feet and slipped Eustace into her pocket. Leaving her room, Rana headed for the library. Duard followed her from her room to the library but did not bother to enter the library. He just took up the guard position outside it. The library had been stuffed into a bedroom, which meant it was all jumbled up. However, Rana could still get at all the books. She started at one side of the room and worked her way along. She studied the titles of each book before moving on to the next one. If any of them looked like it might be what she was looking for, Rana picked it up and flipped through it. She ended up putting them back because none of them were quite what she was looking for. She went through the whole collection of books without finding anything on demons. There were some other books which she was interested in reading, but they would not be helpful to her current situation.

Rana left the library without any books and went back to her room. Duard followed her and took up the position outside her room as she went inside. She took Eustace out of her pocket and left him on the table as she got changed into her nightgown. When she climbed into bed, Eustace settled on the next pillow. Rana expected the creaking to start any time now and just lay there waiting for it.

Would Prince Kenneth figure out that Mar was the hummingbird? What had happened to Mar, which caused her to change so dramatically? Would Isadora and Alim be able to stop Duke Reginald and Monico? Was it indeed true love between Prince Kenneth and Mar? The questions continued to flit across Rana's mind and she wished the book had not disappeared. Briefly, she wondered if the demon had taken her book and what the demon would do with it.

The creaking started and Rana did her best to ignore it. Eustace did not have any problem with the noise because he began to snore. Rana wished she could do the same. It would be much more pleasant than lying there listening to the sounds, especially since her own lover was far away and not coming back. Not that she could fault the couple. They were apparently very much in love and had a healthy relationship. They also did not know they activity could be heard through the ceiling and keeping her up. Hopefully after the renovations, there would be more soundproofing between rooms and floors.

Finally, the noise stopped and Rana closed her eyes. Now she could get some sleep. Suddenly there was moaning coming through the wall from the side which was Rana's maid's room. Rana gave a deep sigh loud enough to disturb Eustace, who glared at her before readjusting himself. Eustace went back to sleep. Rana folded her pillow over her ears and tried to get to sleep.

The next morning after breakfast, Rana found herself outside with the list of ingredients for the herb mixture. Duard was following her around but made no comment on what she was doing. The clover was easy as there was a whole grove of them a short distance from the house. The dandylion took a trip a little further into the forest, but it was still relativity easy to get. There were rose bushes in the garden area though the area was overgrown. This made it harder. Rana tried to get to the rose bushes, but with the crutch, it was almost impossible to get through all the other bushes growing so closely together.

"Would you like some help, Lady Rana?" Duard finally asked.

"Please," Rana answered, "I need a twig from a rose bush."

"Very well," Duard said. He worked his way through the other bushes to the rose bush and being careful of the thorns broke off a twig. He brought it back to her and

Rana placed it in her basket.

"If it is not imposing," Duard said, "May I ask what you are doing, Lady Rana?"

"I have been in communication with Luce," Rana said, "And he is a wizard. He believes that Eustace's reaction to the workman yesterday was a sign that the workman is a demon. However, I do not want to do anything to cause embarrassment if the man should just be a man instead of a demon. So, Luce gave me a recipe with which it is possible to see passed any magical disguises and shows the truth of what is underneath."

"Would you mind if I were to try this recipe as well?" Duard asked.

"You can," Rana answered, "I just need a good enough description of the demon to give to Luce so he can figure out what kind it is and so he can tell me the best way to kill it."

"Seeing this demon will make it easier for me to help you with killing it," Duard said, "Because if my mind believes the demon to be a man, it will fight the urge to kill it. And should it change into its demon form I would not be surprised by its appearance and hesitate when swiftness is necessary.'

"Then Havard should probably also have some," Rana said, "The mixture is supposed to be good for today, but useless tomorrow."

"Havard will be up in time for lunch," Duard said, "If the mixture is still good then, we should not need to wake him."

"Just need two more ingredients," Rana said as she headed toward the garden where Selwyn's daughter-law-in was working. They reached it and the woman looked up at them.

"May I help you, Lady Rana?" the woman asked.

"I hope so," Rana answered, "I need a handful of sage and some leaves from a bean vine."

"Of course," the woman said. She cut a handful of sage for Rana and placed it in the basket. Then the woman gathered some of the leaves from the bean vines she had grown. These she also put in the basket.

"Is there anything else, Lady Rana?" the woman asked.

"No," Rana said, "Thank you for these.

"You are welcome, Lady Rana," the woman said with a curtsy.

Rana headed inside with Duard following her. She went to the kitchen. Breakfast had been cleaned up and preparation for lunch had not started yet. Selwyn's wife, or anyone else, was not in the kitchen. However, it did not take much for Rana to find a pot small enough for her purpose. She put the contents of her basket into it and filled the rest with water. Then Rana put the pot over the fire to let it boil.

Rana went up to her room to get her book and came back down. Duard had stayed in the kitchen in case Selwyn's wife came back and decided to throw out what was in the pot. Rana settled into a chair as she waited for the pot to boil. Duard stood near the door.

The story went into detail about this mystery man and how he had awakened feelings in the widow she had never felt, even with her husband. It went on about how the man seemed to know so much and yet said so little. The widow was always falling over herself whenever he was anywhere around her. She was tongue tied around him and nervous. Rana thought it silly to be unable to speak to someone if you loved them. The ability to talk to someone was part of the relationship. To talk and laugh and enjoy each other's company. The complete opposite of the widow and her mystery suitor. Then the town bully saw the newcomer seemed to have an interest in the woman he was blackmailing into marrying him and he got upset.

Rana put the book down when she went to check on the water, which was starting to boil. She stirred it to make sure the ingredients would spread through the water. Then she went back to the chair to read more of the book as there was nothing more she could do for another half an hour.

The town bully challenged the newcomer to a duel, but the man refused to fight. The widow was sad over this because it meant she would not be able to get out of marrying the town bully. The newcomer did not stop his interest in the widow, but she hesitated in wanting to get too close to a man who was not willing to fight for what he wanted. The newcomer would not answer when she asked why he had refused to fight the duel. The town gossip spread all kinds of things about this newcomer, but no one truly knew anything about him. The widow spent a dozen pages moaning about how awful her life was and how there was nothing she could do about her situation.

Rana put the book down again and went over to the pot. It had been boiling for about half an hour. There was a smell coming off it Rana did not find very appetizing, but she figured it was not meant to be. Like medicine, it would taste awful so it was not abused when it was not needed. Rana poured the liquid into four mugs because that was how much liquid she had. Leaving the mugs to cool, Rana tossed out the ingredients, which were cooking to a mush that definitely did not look edible. Then she sat back down in her chair with her book.

The widow was back to falling in love with the mysterious newcomer despite wanting to label him a coward because aside from choosing not to fight the town bully the newcomer seemed to be brave and willing to help people. The town bully kept trying to keep the widow and the newcomer apart but was not successful in that matter. He did not have control of the widow quite yet because they had not gotten married and the newcomer did not do anything the town bully told him to do. It frustrated the town bully until he decided on a course of action. He announced the date of the wedding for him and the widow. Suddenly she had people needing her time to help her plan the wedding. The seamstress needed some of her time so the dress could be started.

Rana put the book down and checked on the mugs. The liquid was starting to cool but was not even close to the right temperature to drink it. Before Rana could turn to go back to her chair, Selwyn's wife entered the kitchen to start making lunch. She sniffed the air and frowned.

"I am waiting for the water to cool down in these mugs," Rana said as she pointed to the mugs with the liquid in them, "Please do not touch them."

"Yes, Lady Rana," Selwyn's wife said. She started lunch but gave the mug plenty of space to themselves. Rana sat back down to continue reading her book.

The newcomer still found time to visit with the widow and she enjoyed the quiet of his visits in the chaos of wedding planning. The whole town loved big events and this wedding would be one of the biggest and the town bully was willing to pay for things as they were available. That made everyone happy as they pushed the preparations along. As the wedding date got nearer, the widow became more and more nervous which included thoughts of killing herself to avoid marrying such a person. Anyone who noticed thought it was merely the pre-wedding jitters, except the newcomer who for some reason seemed to know more than she had ever told him about the situation.

The wedding was approaching a very fast pace when a pirate showed up; wooden leg, eye patch, and everything. He started following the newcomer around for a couple days and then he spent most of his time at the town tavern trying to drink it dry. The widow avoided the newcomer during the time when he was being followed around by the pirate. When it was over, the newcomer did not explain why the pirate had been following his around even through the widow asked. The widow spent another dozen or more pages conflicted about the newcomer and horrified at her upcoming marriage. Still she could not think of any way out of the situation. Rana wanted to sit the widow down and have a long talk with her about helping herself and not depending on some man to come rescue her.

When Selwyn's wife announced that it was time to eat, Rana checked on the mugs again. They were just about cool, but would probably be the right temperature after lunch. She followed everyone else into the dining room.

When lunch was over, Rana, Duard, and Havard met in the kitchen. They gave space for the people who were helping to clean up but made sure the mugs were not dumped. Selwyn came in and stopped to look at them.

"What is going on?" Selwyn asked.

"We believe that one of the workmen is a demon," Rana said, "And we are about to drink this concoction which is supposed to show through magical disguises."

"A demon?" Selwyn asked looking nervous, "But all of those workers are men I have known for years and would never hurt anyone. They are from the village and were raised there. I hired them because I knew them and knew they were trustworthy."

"I do not know much about demons," Rana said, "But I believe they do have the ability to appear to be someone else. If one of the workmen is a demon than we need to find out what happened to the real person."

"Of course," Selwyn said.

"Perhaps you would like to join us," Rana said, "Then you can tell us about the man who is being impersonated if there is a demon. With that information, we can see what we can do for the man."

"Very well," Selwyn said though he did not look too happy about it.

"As far as I know you just drink the liquid," Rana said, "But I am not sure what happens after that."

The men nodded. Everyone took a cup and drink the contents. It did not taste very good, so they all downed it as fast as they could. Finally, the four mugs were empty and the four stood there. There were no apparent effects from drinking the mixture.

"How do we tell the difference?" Selwyn asked.

"I do not know," Rana answered, "But the best test might be to go outside and watch the workmen."

They headed outside. Rana went to her chair and Havard went with her. Duard and Selwyn found a place to see the workmen from a better angle. Rana watched the workmen for several minutes, but there was no difference from yesterday. However, slowly one of the men became blurry. It was the one Eustace had reacted to.

It was like a screen was taken down from in front of the man and now they could see him clearly. He was the same height as the tallest man, but much thinner. The only clothing he wore was a loincloth around his waist. His skin was a greenish grey. His body shape was the same as the men working beside him though his head and limbs were slight out of proportion from his body. He had three eyes and only slits for nostrils.

Rana looked at Havard, who looked back at her in wonder. Rana took out the paper she had brought with her and started writing down as much of the description of the demon as she could because she did not know how long she would be able to see passed the magical disguise.

"Then what happened to the man?" Havard asked.

"I would suggest we ask for the location of his home and see if we can find the man," Rana said.

"We can discuss it with Duard and Selwyn," Havard said as he looked to where they were on their way over. Duard had Selwyn's elbow to help keep Selwyn on his feet. They reached where Rana and Havard were sitting and Selwyn sat down in the third chair.

"You were right," Selwyn said, "His name is Smithson and he lives with his family on a plot of land on the other side of the village. He is a very hard worked and provides for his family the best he can while they grow vegetables to eat and sell. He has a wife and four children as well as his parents living with them."

"Let us go find his house," Rana said, "Perhaps some of our answers are there."

"I will get the carriage hooked up," Selwyn said. He got shakily to his feet. Duard followed as Selwyn headed for the stable.

"How long will this vision last?" Havard asked.

"I do not know," Rana said.

"Well, if it lasts for our journey to Smithson's home then we will be prepared for anything that might await us," Havard said.

"You are right," Rana said. She continued to watch the workmen and especially the demon. Nothing changed as they continued to watch.

Rana got to her feet when she saw the carriage was ready; Havard joined her as she headed for it. Carter was in the driver's seat while Selwyn had gotten up beside him. Havard and Duard joined Rana inside the carriage. Once they were all settled Carter got the carriage moving while Selwyn gave directions.

It was not far. The house on the plot of land was exactly as Selwyn said; it was on the other side of the village and was a well-cared for house with a large garden. The garden looked like no one had cared for it for a couple days and the house appeared to have been abandoned. Carter parked the carriage on the side of the road in front of the house. Everyone, except Carter, got down. Havard and Duard went ahead as they checked over the property for any traps or enemies. Rana and Selwyn followed at a slower pace to give the guards plenty of time to look things over before they got there.

When they reached the front door, Selwyn knocked. They waited for any response. When none came, Selwyn tried again. And again there was no answer. Rana tried opening the door and found it was easy to open. Duard entered the house first and the rest came in with Havard bringing up the rear.

There was a bedroom on each side of the hallway with two more doorways closer to the back, which were the kitchen and a room for processing the produce. All of the rooms were empty and looked as if the family had just dropped what they were doing and disappeared. It was eerie and uncomfortable. Selwyn became more nervous the more they looked in the rooms and saw no trace of the family.

Rana went out the back door with Havard following her. There were the outhouse and a shed for tools which was leaning against the house. Havard looked into the outhouse. When he pulled his head out, he shook his head to indict to it was empty. Rana opened the door to the shed and stepped inside. It had plenty of room for all the tools along with a large wooden door with handles and a lock.

"Over here," Rana called. Havard looked in and saw the door.

"I will go get the other two," Havard said, "Do not open it."

"I will not," Rana said. Havard left her with the door open. Rana did not try to open it, but she put her ear to the door. She thought she heard someone down there, but she could not be sure.

Havard arrived back with Duard and Selwyn. Then Havard and Duard tried to get the wooden doors open. The lock caused them some problem and they and to resort to using the tools to break the door open. The doors opened into a small cellar, which held what was left of last year's crop as well as Smithson, his wife, their four children, and an older couple who were his parents. They were all alive but tied up. Havard and Duard went into the cellar while Rana and Selwyn waited outside. The guards cut the rope and removed the gags. Then they directed everyone up to the door. Rana and Selwyn helped each person out of the cellar as they were having difficulty with stiff limbs from the lack of movement for too many days.

They got the family out of the shed and provided them with water as they family looked like they had been without. Finally, everyone just sat in the yard and rested.

"What happened?" Selwyn asked Smithson.

"I was getting to meet with the crew to go to work on your project when this thing charged into the house," Smithson said, "I must have knocked out because the next thing I knew we were tied up and in the cellar. I do not know how long we were down there."

"This would be the third day," Selwyn said.

"I thank you all for the rescue," Smithson said, "I thought we would die down there."

"We might not have gone looking for you, but Lady Rana suggested one of the men on the crew was a demon," Selwyn said, "I thought it was nonsense until I drank the potion which showed that you were a demon. I thought you might be dead, but they suggested we come here and check. I am glad we did."

"I am very glad you did too," Smithson said.

"What do we do now?" Havard asked Rana.

"We did not want to tip off the demon that we know," Rana said, "Because if we do, it might change disguises and then we would have to find it again. But it appears we are fortunate enough that the demon did not check on its prisoners. We need to find you a safe place and then I can talk to Luce this evening. Hopefully, he can tell us how to kill the demon once he had the description."

"I know of a safe place for them to go," Selwyn said, "As long as it is not for very long."

"Only until we have dealt with the demon," Rana said, "Then they can go back to life as normal. But everything here has to be exactly as it was when we arrived as I do not know where the demon is resting, if it rests."

"Okay," Selwyn said, "I will get them to the safe place and then head back to the estate."

"Good," Rana said.

"Thank you for the rescue, my lady," Smithson said.

"You are welcome," Rana said.

Then the family gathered themselves together. Selwyn led them off as they went with stiff joints and at a slow walk. Once they were out of sight, Havard and Duard made sure everything was as when they arrived. Then together with Rana they got back in the carriage. Carter drove them back to the estate.

When she was dropped off on the steps with Havard, Rana looked over at the workmen and found she could still see the demon instead to Smithson. She went inside. She spent the rest of the afternoon reading while Havard stood guard outside her door.

The widow woke up the morning of the wedding and did not have time to worry or be nervous because someone wanted her attention for the moment they knew she had woken up right to the moment the wedding was supposed to start. Actually, she had five minutes to sit there and get nervous as she sat in one of the small rooms off the foyer of the church as she waited for the ceremony to start. Her attendants were helping deal with any finishing touches, so she was left alone. That was when the newcomer showed up to visit her. He asked whether she loved him and she was forced to admit that yes she did. He asked her why she was marrying the town bully and she had to admit that he was blackmailing her into it though she did not tell him what the blackmail was. Then he assured her that he would stop the wedding before disappearing.

Shortly after the newcomer had left, her attendants came to get her. The ceremony started and the widow kept expecting the newcomer to burst in and break up the wedding, but he never did. The priest gave a little sermon and then went through the vows without the newcomer stopping the wedding. The town bully was in full confidence now because everything was going exactly as he planned. She would be his and she would not be able to do anything about it.

Then the priest called for those who objected to the

union to speak up. The newcomer got to his feet and announced he objected because no one should be forced into a marriage which was not based in love, but in greed on one side. The townspeople were silent while the town bully got red in the face as he lost his temper. He shot back that the newcomer had tried to steal the widow since they had gotten engaged and it was out of petty jealousy causing him to stand up and make false statements. The town bully shut up when the newcomer claimed the right of the duel, which the town bully could not decline because he had issued it.

They proceeded to have the duel right there in the church. The newcomer won because he caused the town bully to surrender and give up his plans to marry the widow. Then the newcomer asked for the widow's hand in marriage, which she agreed to. They were married and the festivities resumed. There was the feast and the dance. The town bully went home to lick his wounds. Finally at the end of the night, the newcomer told the widow that he was a ship's captain and asked her to come with him and his first mate, who was the pirate who showed up earlier. She said yes and they left town on a broken down all cart singing old sea chanties.

After supper, Rana returned to her room and sat down in her chair. She took the communication crystal in both her hands to warm it up as fast as she could. In half the time it started to cloud and Rana changed it to just holding the communication crystal in one hand. Luce's face slowly appeared.

"The herb mixture worked," Rana said.

"Good," Luce said, "Did you get a good description of the demon?"

"It is tall and thin with greenish grey skin," Rana said,

"It only wore a loincloth and looks mostly human; though it had three eyes and not much of a nose. It eyes were a similar shade to his skin."

"Okay," Luce said, "Just give me a moment." There was quiet with only the sound of flipping pages and the image of Luce had its head down. Eustace was sitting on the table in front of Rana and he titled his head to one side and looked up at her as if wondering what was going on. Finally, Luce looked up.

"From the description the demon is called a Firgy," Luce said, "It is classified as intelligent. Usually, it is hired by something else to put the scheme into action, but it also hires itself out as an assassin. It is a close to a human as demons come. The only magic it uses is what it uses to disguise itself as a person close to its intended victim. Swords are the best option to deal with such demons though any weapon should work. However, it is best to burn the body because otherwise they have been known to come back after few days and go back to work. It does not nest, but will find a new hiding place when it needs to rest. Its primary food source in plants and it does not eat meat unless it has to in order to maintain its disguise. Any other questions about it?"

"Does it eat books?" Rana asked.

"What?" Luce asked.

"Never mind," Rana said, "Thank you for the information."

"I hope it is useful in dealing with the demon," Luce said.

"I am sure it will be," Rana said.

"If you need me you can contact me via the communication crystal," Luce said.

"I will," Rana said, "Good night."

"Good night," Luce said and then he disappeared

from the crystal. Rana placed the crystal on the table beside Eustace, who looked at her expectantly. She stared at the fire for a long time as she thought about it.

Rana's thoughts were interrupted when her maid came into the room. She looked up at her maid. Her maid started any cleaning she did in the evening, including putting out Rana's nightgown. Rana went back to staring into the fire as her mind kept working.

When Rana's maid had finished the cleaning, she started for the door.

"Ask Havard, Duard, and Selwyn to meet me in the dining room in half an hour," Rana said. Her maid looked at her for a moment in confusion.

"Yes, Lady Rana," her maid said finally. She left the room.

Eustace raised his head from being curled up as he had gotten bored of waiting for Rana to say something. She looked at him and smiled.

"I think I know how to trap the demon," Rana said, "All I have to do it get the men to agree to my plan." Rana reached out her hand and Eustace crawled on to it. She slipped him into her pocket. Then she left her room. Duard was standing guard at her door. He left his position and followed her as she headed for the dining room.

They reached the dining room as the first ones there and sat down. Havard joined them next. Before Selwyn arrived, his wife brought in tea for everyone along with a plate of cookies. She took a seat and then her husband joined them. He did not look happy about her being there.

"I have a right to know what is happening," Selwyn's wife told him, "This is my home too."

"I do not think I have heard your name," Rana said.

"My name is Felice, Lady Rana," Selwyn's wife replied.

"You are more than welcome here, Felice," Rana said. Selwyn still did not look happy, but he did not try to say anything more about it.

"I do not know what your husband has told you," Rana said, "But the situation is this. One of the workmen is a demon in disguise. We rescued him and his family earlier today, but we are trying to keep that quiet as we want him to keep the same disguise as it is much easier to kill it when we know who it is. The experiment with the liquid this morning was to see if we could see through the demon's disguise and it worked. We know the demon is Smithson and now we need to discuss how to deal with the demon in such a way as no one else gets hurt."

"Okay," Felice said, "That does make sense."

"What did you find out about the demon?" Havard asked.

"It hires itself as an assassin," Rana answered, "It does not nest and the magic it uses is to disguise itself. The best weapon against it is a sword, which it reacts in a similar way as a human would. And if you do not burn the body it will come back after a few days."

"The fire pit out back can be used as a pyre," Felice said, "Though it might take some time to get the fire to the right temperature to burn the body properly."

"But if we try to attack the demon when the men arrive for work the rest of the workmen will be very upset and try to stop us," Duard said, "They will see it as attacking one of their own."

"I do not want the demon to be attacked near the other workmen," Rana said, "That would be too dangerous and people may get hurt unnecessarily."

"Except the workmen arrive together, work together all day, and then leave together," Selwyn said, "They are never separate and when they are it is not for very long."

"We need to make sure we can get him separated from the rest of the men," Rana said, "We also have to do this without raising his suspicion because if he gets away from us, then he can change disguises and more people get hurt. I was thinking Selwyn would be the best person to lead him away from the others as Selwyn is the main person the group has been dealing with and it will look more natural."

"Maybe a discussion about buying some produce from Smithson's family," Felice said, "It would be a natural thing for them to talk about and no one would think twice about it."

"That would be good," Rana said.

"But the demon thinks Smithson's family is trapped in the cellar," Selwyn said.

"The demon does not care about that," Rana said, "I think it will have the conversation with you to make his disguise look natural."

"Okay," Selwyn said, "But where do I lead him?"

"To the kitchen door," Rana said, "Because that is where you are expected to lead him and the discussion would be held. Duard will be sitting with me and Havard will be coming out of the kitchen for some fresh air. Both normal things. When the right moment arrives, they will attack the demon. Once the demon appears to be dead, we will put him in the fire pit. After which we will have to explain things to the workmen. When it is finished burning, we scatter the ashes as far as we can."

"Sounds good," Duard said.

"How are we going to explain the fire to the workmen?" Havard asked, "They may ask, they may not."

"We are getting to fire ready to properly roast a pig," Felice answered.

"Then the plan is good to me," Havard said.

"I suppose it will have to do," Selwyn said.

"I will start the fire when I get up tomorrow morning," Felice said, "Then it will be ready about the time the workmen come. Selwyn will have to start the conversation early in the day because otherwise it might look suspicious as it is rude to interrupt the work later in the day."

"Then I believe we are set," Rana said, "I will see everyone in the morning."

Everyone said goodnight as Rana got to her feet. She left the dining room and headed back to her room. Both the guards stayed, likely to discuss anything else for tomorrow. She was not in danger in the house at night time and if there were some danger, Eustace would be a good warning system.

Reaching her room, Rana changed into her nightgown. Eustace was curled up on the next pillow when she crawled into bed. She closed her eyes and tried not to think of the excitement of tomorrow. And tonight she was in bed early, so hopefully she would get to sleep before anything could prevent it. With that, she started to drift off. Rana was not that far into sleep when the creaking started. She groaned and folded her pillow over her head.

TAKING CARE OF THE DEMON AND WHAT HAPPENS AFTER THAT

When the workmen arrived the next morning, there was a large fire burning in the fire pit and everyone except Selwyn was ready. Selwyn knew his part, but he was still nervous about the whole thing. Rana was starting to wonder if he was not the right person for the job, but it was too late to change it now. She would just have to hope Selwyn could do it without tipping the demon off that there was something wrong.

Rana was sitting in her usual chair with a book in her hand. She had been reading it when the workmen arrived. She expected to see them all as workmen, but instead she could still see the demon rather than Smithson. Duard was sitting in the next chair and was in his usual posture. From looking at them, you would not guess anything unusual was going to happen.

Some of the men stopped to look at the fire, but the

talk among themselves seemed to give them a satisfactory answer. They started to work. Rana saw Selwyn come out and talked to the foreman for a couple minutes. Then he went over to the demon and said something while waving toward the kitchen door. The demon was agreeable to whatever was said.

They started walking toward the kitchen door. Selwyn kept talking, but it must have been typical gossip because the demon gave no sign he noticed anything unusual. Of course, he seemed to be spacing out rather than listening so the topic of conversation held no interest for him. When they were half way to the kitchen door, Havard stepped out of it. He appeared to just be out for a stroll. Duard got up and started walking toward Havard as if he had something they needed to discuss. Both appeared to be paying no attention to Selwyn and the demon. The kitchen door was far enough from the workmen they could not see what was happening there unless they were taking stuff to the pile.

Rana found herself holding her breath as she peeked over her book. She tried to relax by letting the breath out quietly and taking in a deep breath just as quietly. The last thing she wanted was for her to be the one to give everything away. If this did not work, no one knew what the demon would do.

Then Selwyn arrived, where Havard and Duard had stopped, with the demon. They both pulled their swords out and attacked. Selwyn ducked and ran for cover away from the fight. The demon took out a knife and blocked Duard's sword while avoiding Havard's sword. Both kept swinging and attacking. The demon was faster and slightly stronger than an average human. Castle guards are not always the best as far as trained soldiers went. However, with two against one the fight was about even.

Finally, one of Havard's slashed reached the demon and cut through its skin. This left a tear a skin hanging down, but there was no blood to go along with it. It did not slow the demon down much, but it act like it was injured. This made it much easier for Duard and Havard. The some of the next several slashes reached the demon and made the same marks on the demon as the first one. Each time the demon slowed down a little bit.

Then Duard swung at the demon's neck. The demon was too busy trying to dodge Havard's sword and did not see the second sword swing. There was a strange noise as the head separated from the body. It was sort of like a half strangled scream. It was enough to bring the workmen. Duard and Havard were putting their swords away and Selwyn was coming out of his hiding place.

The workmen were upset about Smithson disappearing and demanded answers. Selwyn was apparently calm enough to explain everything because shortly the workmen were helping Duard and Havard carry the body over to the fire pit. The body was laid in the fire and then everyone stepped back. Rana had put her book down and just watched everything. She watched the flames lick at the body as if seeing if it was any good to eat and then they jumped to the body as if they found the most delicious thing ever. As the body was engulfed in the flames, Rana was sure she could see it twitching.

Rana, Duard, and Havard stayed and watched the body burn. The workmen went back to the renovating project. Selwyn went off to tell Smithson that his family was safe, the demon was gone, and he could come to work when he was ready. Felice came out a couple times to check the fire and to add more wood when it needed it. Only once the body was no longer recognizable did Rana go inside to read her book. Felice had taken over dealing with the body and ashes, so there was no worry there.

After supper, Rana went up to her room without any guard to stand at her door. She went inside and took Eustace out of her pocket. Eustace took up residence on the table as usual. He had been feed extra tonight as Felice had noticed him and asked about him. Rana had more than willing to talk about her pet and Eustace was always willing to accept the plate of food put in front of him.

Rana sat down in the chair and picked up the communication crystal. She held it in her palm as she waited for it to warm up. Luce had not said anything about wanting to know the outcome, but that was not all she wanted to talk to him about. Slowly the heat from her hand seeped into the communication crystal. When it was warm enough, the smooth part got cloudy and Luce came into focus.

"How did the demon slaying go?" Luce asked.

"It went well," Rana answered, "It is now ash in the wind."

"That is a good place for it to be," Luce said, "Was anyone injured?"

"No," Rana answered, "But I think my guards are going to need some more training of they are going to stick around."

"Are you worried about such things happening again?" Luce asked, "Or just think they need better training?"

"Both," Rana said, "My carriage was passing through a market on the way to the country estate and a woman offered to tell my fortune. Eustace got between me and her while hissing and such. Her eyes turned red and then she hurried away. Whatever she was it was different than the demon my guards killed today. That means there are more out there and I seem to be one of their targets. If that is the case then I need to learn as much as I can about demons and my guards need to be much better trained than having to have two of them to take out one demon."

"That does make sense," Luce said.

"So, I need you to teach me everything you can about demons," Rana said.

"I suppose I can do that," Luce said, "Since it seems you will need the information. As soon as I can I will send some books on demons to you for studying. We can also schedule time when we doing some training over the communication crystal. I can send someone who is really good at fighting to see if it is any help in training your guards."

"I would appreciate that as I do not know anyone I could ask to do it," Rana said, "I know you have other things to do, but I think this might be the difference between life or death."

"I am willing to teach you as much as I can," Luce said, "But I am no expert in demons."

"That is all right," Rana said, "I just need enough that I know what to do the next time one shows up."

"Okay," Luce said, "I will send those books as soon as I can and we can talk about the schedule soon. I am still working on getting myself out of a sticky situation so I may not have much time until then.'

"I have nothing to so but sit here and study," Rana said, "So, whenever you are ready."

"Okay," Luce said, "Use the communication crystal in three days to talk to me and we will see what we can set up."

"Good," Rana said.

"Good night," Luce said, "And good work." Then he disappeared. Rana put the crystal back on the table and picked up her book to continue to read.

TEN MONTHS LATER

Rana sat by the fire in her room and held her sleeping daughter in her arms. Normally Rana would have a book in her hand as well, but tonight she was content to just sit and watch the flames. The construction on the house had been finished and her new suite was plenty big enough for her and her daughter in the corner of the right wing. On the floor below her rooms was a storage area. Selwyn had wondered why Rana had demanded a storage area build there, but she was not going to educate him on the matter. Felice appreciated the storage space without questioning why Rana wanted it. There had been two other demons showed up, but with Rana's education into demons and her guards working with someone who was really good with a sword they were not really a problem. Her guards were now paid by her as they both finished their time with the castle guard and they chose to keep working for Rana. It was pleasant at the country estate; even not everyone was ready for Rana's daughter's arrival.

They now enjoyed the child's presence.

There was a knock at the door.

"Come in," Rana called. A blacksmith could be working out in the hallway and it would not wake her daughter up, so she was not worried about calling out. Duard stepped inside. He was wearing his armour, so he must have been on watch. In his hand was a letter.

"A royal messenger just delivered this," Duard said, "He is in the kitchen getting his supper and Selwyn has prepared a room for him as he seems to expect to send back a reply."

"Thank you, Duard," Rana said as she held out her hand. Duard put the letter in her hand before leaving the room. Rana opened the letter. It was from her brother.

My sister, Rana,

I hope you are well as you have not sent much for letters since you moved out to the country estate. Hillel's war has had various complications here. We have been trying to sort everything out since the missive from Grackle arrived to announce Hillel's execution. Arabella gave birth to a healthy baby boy and named him Waldemar. She has forbidden anyone from talking about Hillel in Waldemar's presence until Waldemar is of the age where he understands his father's crimes against the kingdom.

With this news, I was hoping you were still in contact with Luce. He is the only one we could think of who has magical knowledge. If he is available, maybe he can come help us with a slight problem left from Hillel's rein. He would be paid well for any inconvenience coming would cause.

I have taken over running the kingdom. It is a hard job, but I have been doing pretty much the job for a while now so it was not a big leap. The only difference is that I am now the official leader with the public end of it as well as the running of it. So far I think I can handle it, but it will be nice when Waldemar is of age to take it over.

Daniella sends greetings. She says you need to write to her more, or she is going to steal a carriage and go find you. I think she misses you. Aside from a few complicates from Hillel's rein it is quiet here and that makes for less exciting things happening.

Anyway, I hope you are well and I hope to hear from you soon about Luce.

Your brother, Weldon

Rana put the letter down on the table beside. She went back to gazing into the flames as she thought over what her brother's letter said. The next time she was scheduled to talk to Luce was a couple weeks away. It did not sound like Weldon had that much time if he had given orders to the messenger to wait for the reply.

The door opened and Rana's maid stepped inside.

"I need to tell Duard and Havard that we need to meet in the dining room in half an hour," Rana said before her maid could start her chores.

"Is there something wrong, Lady Rana?" her maid asked.

"Yes, we need to pack up and be ready to leave at first light tomorrow," Rana answered, "My brother has a demon problem at the castle."

"I will let Duard and Havard know right away," her maid left the room. Rana kissed the top of her daughter's head before trying to get up without waking the girl.

CONCLUSION?

There was a knock on the door as Mitchell put the book down. Mitchell glanced at the clock and realized he missed breakfast. The knock was likely to be a servant telling him that his appointment had arrived.

"Come in," Mitchell called. The door opened and the housekeeper stepped into the room.

"A message has arrived for you," the housekeeper said. She came over and offered him the envelope. Mitchell took it. The housekeeper left the study and closed the door behind her. Mitchell opened the envelope and read the message. It was from Thompson, the person Mitchell was expecting. Thompson was sending the message to apologize for not being able to make the meeting this morning but hoped to be able to come that afternoon. If there was a problem with that, Mitchell could just send him a message saying so, otherwise Thompson would just assume it was okay to come.

Mitchell looked at the box of books and the one in his

hand. Maybe he would get Thompson to date them while he was here discussing his own problem. Then Mitchell could tell their age, rather than just guessing they were as old as they looked. Since he had found the box in the hole behind the wall of his new bookshelf, Mitchell was sure there was something to them. Some of the stories seemed closer to fiction than reality while some matched stories his grandfather told.

Mitchell shook his head as he stood up. Of course, these books were fiction. They did not match the history as he had been taught it in school. And if you could not believe your teachers, who could you believe? A grandfather? Mitchell put the book back. He thought about breakfast for a brief moment and then took out the next book. He sat back in his chair, got comfortable, and opened the book.

ABOUT THE AUTHOR

Heather Mantler is a lover of fairy tales and fables. Her home town is Prince George, British Columbia. Heather is always working on another story as she hopes to finish every story idea that she has ever written down. She was a nominee for the fiction category of the 2012 Prince George Regional Arts and Cultural Awards and short listed for the 2013 John Harris Fiction Awards. Her blog is heathersdomain.wordpress.com. Heather encourages her readers to post reviews on Good Reads and Amazon.

www.ingramcontent.com/pod-product-compliance
Lightning Source LLC
Chambersburg PA
CBHW060936050726
47592CB00003B/983